Th  Terrorist

Jeffrey Sabins

Published by Jeffrey Sabins

© 2019

All rights reserved. No part of this book
may be reproduced or modified in any
form, including photocopying,
recording, or by any information storage
and retrieval system, without permission
in writing from the publisher.

ISBN: 9781689161367

DEDICATION

This book is dedicated to one of the best units I have had the honor of serving with. In 2006, fighting in Ramadi, Iraq with 3B of Weapons Company, 3rd Battalion, 8th Marines had to be the toughest and greatest months of my life. To each and every warrior, thanks for being the strongest, wisest, and most elite bad-ass men I have ever known.

ACKNOWLEDGMENTS

My wife Kelli Sabins has been the greatest influence in making this dream come true. Without her, this story would have been stuck inside my head until Vahalla!

Legend

IED[1] a simple bomb made and used by unofficial or unauthorized forces

POGS[2] these are known as a form of money on military camps overseas. Reducing the need of members to carry actual coins, they are face value according to their picture

COC[3] combat Operations Center, the command post for a combat arms unit

EOD[4] explosive ordnance disposal (EOD) technicians, who are specially trained to deal with the construction, deployment, disarmament, and disposal of high explosive munitions

RIP[5] relief-in-place/transfer of authority of unit

<u>CHAPTER ONE</u>

The Beginning

<u>*August 11th 2019*</u>

He was already feeling mentally and physically drained. Preparing for this upcoming challenge has been difficult, but Gunnery Sergeant Jared Tremble knew exactly what needed to be done. It was decided a long time ago that enough was enough. He knew it was time he took matters into his own hands.

It wasn't a hard decision, at least when focusing on himself as an individual. When he starts to think about his family, it will never get easier. The possibility of leaving his children forever often makes him question the choice he has ultimately made.

The decision is final and there is no turning back. He had already taken the necessary steps to achieve his ultimate goal. There was no stopping the impact of those measures he had already taken. Jared, who is a 15 year seasoned Marine Corps Infantryman, was attached to the Task Force 151. The 14,000 Marines he had deployed with over the years never would have foreseen their beloved leader they once knew, side with the most ruthless and barbaric terrorist organization, The Army of Islam.

Growing up in a small town in upstate New York, Jared was always the quiet individual who mostly kept to himself. He didn't enjoy going out to parties with friends or hanging out after school. There were more important things to take care of. He needed to be cutting wood for the stove during the winter, hunting to stock the freezer, and protecting his younger brother who often got bullied.

Their parents have been divorced for quite some time, it had always been them against the world. They did everything together and often made plans about what adventures they would get into when they grew older. The two brothers spent many of their days side by side.

With one red light in the entire town, not a single fast food restaurant or shopping mall, there wasn't much to do but work and play sports. Without many friends, Jared stuck to high school wrestling and doing work around the house for his father. It made the time go by and kept Jared in great shape. There was no interest in anything else, nothing that called out Jared's name. At one point in his life he dreamed of pursuing the sport in college, but that was a young boys dream.

The small family modular home appeared to be dropped in the middle of the town cemetery. Coming from the main road in town, someone visiting the family would never expect such a small house to be down the long driveway. There was no epic mountain view, or waterfront access. There were headstones of loved ones gone, but never forgotten. Hundreds of them, as far as the eyes could see through the sloping hills.

This likely had something to do with the small amount of friends Jared had. When looking outside the box and looking at the big picture of Jared's life, spending all that time alone or with his brother likely helped Jared in his career as an infantryman. Knowing how to survive and getting by on his own was a great factor in getting through Marine Corps boot camp and the multiple combat tours throughout his career.

Jared had never dreamed of being a Marine, not like the typical stories you hear. He was 5'11" and almost 130 pounds. Jared enjoyed wrestling throughout highschool, so he was used to shedding weight instead of putting it on. He was skinny, with red hair and blue eyes. Jared didn't look like a typical Marine.

He often had thoughts on going to college and being a conservation officer, but only because he enjoyed being outside as often as possible. Those thoughts were short lived, but was it external forces or just pure impulse that lead Jared to his future. On February 12th 2004, he was having another normal day. Getting to his lunch period, he saw a Marine Corps Recruiter set up on a small stage in the corner of the cafeteria. Jared had walked over to speak with him out of pure curiosity, but within just five minutes he had started the application process. There was nothing unique or extremely motivating that caught his attention, it was just something to do.

Many members of the family have an idea that Jared just wanted to get out of the small town life and become a new person. To create a new image for himself, but Jared would never confirm nor deny that narrative. Within just a few days, his parents signed the papers to allow him to join the Marine Corps at 17 years old. One week later he had a date to ship off to Marine boot camp. Three months after that, Jared walked across his high school stage to receive his diploma. Within an hour of graduating, he was walking out of the school and into the recruiters car, which took him straight to the airport for boot camp.

While at boot camp in South Carolina, Jared often kept to himself. He was fine when it came to the physical training aspect, had more difficulty with drill and following directions. Twice, Jared was "physically corrected" during his time attending bootcamp. The first time was when they transitioned from shoes to boots and Jared went ahead and bloused his trousers straight into his boots. The second was when Jared leaned over to get closer to his short Senior Drill Instructor because he couldn't hear him.

After boot camp, Jared traveled to North Carolina to the School of Infantry to pick a skill, or Military Occupational Specialty. He didn't have a high enough GT score for some of the occupations, so he ended up choosing machine guns since he was decent at hiking and carrying weight. It took some time, but Jared eventually became adapted to machine gunnery and had some of the fastest times during drills. He was hooked.

Jared was a machine gunner in Fallujah and Ramadi Iraq from 2004 and 2006. After a quick six months on ship, Jared eventually went to Marjah, Afghanistan and then to the Horn of Africa for a few more years of fighting. Jared was definitely battle tested, he had proven himself to be a ferocious fighter and keen survivor. Jared had put on 60 pounds of muscle and a never dulling savage look in his eyes.

He walked with a sense of earned confidence from years of fighting. In his fifteen years as an infantry Marine, he had been shot three times, hit by over nineteen IED's$_1$ while traveling in armored vehicles, and had been through more firefights than family cookouts.

Jared had never expected it, but he was a great Marine, good at fighting and pushing others to fight harder. He enjoyed deploying and wanted to fight as often as possible. Highly decorated and a passion for leading Marines in combat, Jared was born for this.

Nonetheless, these instincts would be tested even further once this next step was taken. Nothing could prepare him for what was about to happen, but it needed to occur. Countless hours have been used to prepare and plan out his future attempt to join The Army of Islam.

He had fought against them for countless years and knew everything about them. He had spent the last year extensively learning their language fluently. He studied their religion, tactics, and their way of life. How they eat, sleep, and how they evolved culturally. He was prepared, or at least that's what he continued to tell himself.

His bags were packed, his route was planned, and he was in a position to make this happen. He helped develop and build the last three patrol bases in Ramadi and knew everything about each one. This would be his ticket in and how he would prove his loyalty.

Each small camp had a specific military operation plan and Jared had copies of all three in his bag. Presenting these to the leader of The Army of Islam would be his ticket in. None of the Marines in the Task Force knew of his plan. In order to make a scene for a distraction, he had just gotten into a large confrontational argument with the company First Sergeant on the other side of the camp. That of course, would stir up some whispering throughout the base. With the Marines telling others that they saw the Gunny arguing with the First Sergeant on the South side of camp, this would be a great alibi.

No one would expect him to be on the North side of the base, near post four. They had just finished building the structure earlier and it had not yet been implemented in the security plan. Jared would be able to quietly slip through the unsecured post and make his way to his planned objective. The more silent and unnoticed he could be when leaving, the better chance he had of reaching his goal.

All he had to do was take the first step in the blacked-out darkness. He would follow his illuminated compass to the building he had picked out months ago and wait. One step would change his life. One step to take matters in his own hands and join a different cause, to make a change.

He was tired of how things were going and frustrated by all the fighting that led nowhere. His anxiety was rising again and he could feel the anger swell back up inside of him. It was time, there was no reason to wait any longer. No one could see him, no one knew his location, and no one to hold him back. It was his one chance to end it all.

Jared looked around one last time and took the first step to a new life, as an American Terrorist.

<u>CHAPTER TWO</u>

The Encounter

<u>*August 11th 2019*</u>

After twenty minutes of walking in complete darkness, Jared was certain he was approaching where he needed to be. He had planned this route for the last four months. He knew the terrain well. Jared had tagged along on several aerial reconnaissance missions that were routed to fly over this area. He only asked to join to use that time to capture recordings. It was simple to do, as standard procedure stated additional recording devices could be mounted for investigative purposes.

He just happened to conduct his pre inspection on the recording device while flying, turning it on earlier than the others. Once they returned, he played the recording in his room and made his plans in silence. This was one of the perks of having his own living quarters on camp.

After volunteering for two foot patrols, Jared had the pace count developed. He paid attention and memorized the terrain features he needed to follow. With his personally designed ranger bead set, he had the exact number of beads needed for his paces. The design had 43 beads, that he crushed after each time he walked one hundred paces.

Jared used a clay mineral composed of hydrated magnesium silicate that originated in a powder form. Once hydrated, he formed the substance around a string and then dehydrated it. This allowed Jared to create a non traceable device to assist him in keeping his pace count while walking in complete darkness.

Using this personally designed pace counting device, he could crush a bead every one hundred steps. The bead would turn into powder with enough force and blow away with the breeze. He didn't want to get to his location and have a pocket full of beads, but he also didn't want to leave beads on the ground behind him as a trail.

The complete silence of the dark night was deafening, spooking even him. He could never be sure what each step would result in. This drives even the hardest warriors into a lunatic stage. Each step could be his last, any mistake by stepping on a pressure plate could cause a sudden detonation, but he continued on anyway. Jared had nothing to lose at this point in his life. Nothing to return to but hatred and guilt. So he continued on walking through the night.

The darkness began to somehow get even darker ahead, as if a large building was blocking what little light there could be. Jared knew he was arriving soon. Ten more steps and he would be at the location he had chosen. It was in a prime geographical location. Being careful, Jared knew at this point he was already being watched. Without a weapon or uniform, he had hoped this would prevent the usual shoot first and ask later mindset known of the organization. He heard nothing and decided to continue on.

He had often wondered how their first encounter would go. Besides, he was here to befriend them, to switch sides and join their cause. They had to be intelligent enough to realize the potential gain they could obtain from this. Having an American, a Marine willing to share secrets and military building plans from the camps around the area was a good thing for the Army of Islam.

From previous encounters, throughout different battles he had fought through, he knew The Army of Islam had smart leaders. Tactical brilliance that was showcased in ambushes and planned operations throughout the world. In this case, he wasn't worried about the leaders. Instead he was concerned of the loyalist that only follow orders and tend not to think outside the box.

Jared didn't want to get killed before the journey ever got started. How could he ever convince them he had chosen to switch sides if he was already dead on the ground. If he could survive until morning, they would know his intentions for sure. He had made sure of that back at camp.

Jared finally reached the front door of the building. It was a small hut made of sun-dried mud brick. From the outsider perspective, it appeared to be the remnants of an old shop in the middle of the desert. However, nobody worked there or hung around it anymore. A few people come and go from inside, but never a routine.

Jared had learned long ago that this was a place of interest, only because of the constant repairs. There are dozens of worn down abandoned buildings throughout the city, most which have shrapnel and bullet holes through them. None of them are ever repaired, except for this one. Although the outside looks like the rest, the inside is immaculate. Patches are constantly added and the inside stays spotless.

Even after there was an incident three months ago where a short round from a 60 millimeter mortar landed 150 feet in front of it. The building had been shredded with metal. Two weeks later, when Jared was on patrol, he happened to walk inside, alone, to check it out.

The inside was patched and clean. Lights were working from solar panels hidden on top of the building and there appeared to be no internal damage visible. This immediately sparked interest within Jared, especially when he started his own personal mission. Throughout the next few weeks, Jared continued to monitor the camera system inside the Command Operations Center.

As Jared finally reached the front door, he calmly walked inside and sat down in a chair. He had made it all this way without stepping on an explosive device and he was grateful. He took a few moments to enjoy that aspect and then began to carry on. He took off his backpack and laid everything out on the floor. This included two blueprints for Patrol Base (PB) Westie and Patrol Base (PB) Kelly. The third one he had hidden within a secret flap within the bag.

He also laid out some snacks, his water and a letter he had written that explained what he was trying to accomplish. He already knew that when the inevitable began, it would be fast paced with little communication. Jared sat back down in his chair and began to prepare himself. He knew what was next to come.

Jared had been sitting in the same chair for two hours when he began to hear muffled noises. His heart began to race, as the anxiety picked up from the confrontation that was about to occur. Daylight was in three hours, so he assumed everything would go fast. Finally, he could hear a vehicle approaching and slowly come to a stop. There were no lights, but the soft noise of tires sliding and doors closing.

Jared put his hands up and his head down, as the door to the building slammed open and men began to rush in. Two of the younger gentlemen began to scream at him with AK-47's, jabbing at his head. He remained calm and kept his hands raised. He noticed an older gentleman in the back of the room, looking around on the floor at the items Jared had placed out. He didn't act too interested, as he stood and watched the ordeal play out. Could Jared have misplayed his cards from the very beginning?

The two younger fighters were still screaming and one hit Jared with some force with his weapon muzzle. Jared could feel the steady stream of blood starting to run down the right side of his head, but he dared not move. Instead, he held his hands up and began to speak in their native tongue, Mesopotamian Arabic. Ensuring that he spoke slowly and deliberately, Jared began to attempt to speak to the older man in the back, the obvious leader.

"I am not here to cause problems," said Jared, "I only wish to speak with a leader and explain my situation."

No response from the older gentleman, only a blank stare. Jared at least expected a reaction from him when he spoke to them in their language. He received no such attention. Not even a blink of his eyes, this man had obviously seen his fair share of fighting in his lifetime. More screaming and yelling from the other two, still waving their weapons around with no concern of what they impact. Jared decided to test his luck and try again.

"Please, I have important information to share with you and wish to explain my intentions. You can see that I have already graciously provided you with….."

Jared was cut off, as the door opened and three other individuals walked in. Jared had not heard the second vehicle pull up due to the screaming inside the building. It appeared to be getting more serious and Jared hadn't decided if his fate was heading in the right direction just yet.

Now there were four men with guns screaming at him, with two other men in the back discussing something in whispers. The original man from the back suddenly turned towards his two men and snapped his fingers, one aimed at each individual. He pointed towards the door, as if motioning for the vehicle. Both immediately went outside, as the man in charge pulled out a knife.

This was it, Jared thought to himself. All of this planning, only to get stabbed while sitting in this chair. He might be able to fight him off, but the other three were still inside and surely they would shoot first if Jared began to move. He didn't have much of a choice, he was outnumbered. The old man stepped towards Jared, but instead of the life ending jab, he walked past Jared and began to cut the black curtain from the wall. The knife was sharp and he quickly had a decent sized dark sheet in his hand. He slowly and quietly spoke to Jared.

"Put your hands down by your side and do not make fast movements. If you try anything that we deem as a threat, I will cut your throat before you take a second breath. Do you understand?"

Jared nodded his head, "I do," he replied.

Without hesitation, the man immediately wrapped the dark sheet around Jared's face and tied a rope around his neck. It wasn't enough to choke him, but still uncomfortable. Someone grabbed his shoulders and lifted him up off of the seat. They began to push him forward, likely out of the door and towards the vehicle.

"Where are you taking me," Jared asked quietly?

"No more talking, we are taking you with us until we it is decided what to do with you. We will discuss your intentions with the tribal leader who will ultimately make the decision of whether you live, or die. Let's move before I make the decision myself," came the reply.

Underneath the sheet, Jared was smiling. He had successfully survived his first encounter and was on his way in!

CHAPTER THREE

Flashback #1

July 8th 2018

Jared was sitting at his kitchen table, speaking with his wife of 12 years Katie. Jared and Katie had met through a mutual friend, while he was visiting in Tennessee. Through circumstances with being in the Marine Corps, this relationship would not have normally been initiated.

A young man from upstate New York and young woman from a small town in Tennessee, there is no telling if their paths would have ever crossed without the Marine Corps being involved. Jared was extremely happy that their paths had crossed though, as he could not imagine his life any other way right now.

When Jared first met Katie, he never imagined a person like her had even existed. He fell madly in love with her from the very beginning. She had a kind face, with eyes so intriguing and beautiful that there were times ten years down the road that he still could not look away.

She had this unique way of looking amazing in every possible way. Whether it be a summer dress, formal wear, or even sweat pants and a t-shirt, Jared was always stunned by the way she looked. There was never a doubt in his mind that he wasn't madly in love with her and that only proved more true when they had children.

They had two children, their ten year old son Cayden and their eight year old daughter Kaylee. Cayden had proved to be the toughest young man that Jared had ever met. When Cayden was two in 2011, the Naval Hospital Emergency Room had discovered that there was a peach size tumor within his brain.

Within minutes of discovery, Cayden was packed in a medical helicopter and flown three hours west to a major children's hospital. This initiated

Cayden being admitted thirty six days and going through three major brain surgeries. Also, at the age of five, Cayden additionally was diagnosed with autism. Now ten, he had been through so much in his lifetime, but still found a way to wake up every single morning with the biggest smile on his face.

Kaylee was full of life and never had a dull moment. With a sparkle in her eye that never disappeared, she had plans on being the center of attention since day one. To this day, Jared still says Kaylee was born wearing a fancy dress. She was always doing something girly, whether it would be dancing, cheerleading, or gymnastics. She had a major love for animals and planned on being a veterinarian when she grew up. Her super power, was the ability to make friends with every soul she encountered.

Jared loved his family, even dreamed of spending every moment he could with them when he finally got out of the military, but he also loved fighting. His love hate relationship with deployments created frustration for his family, especially his wife. This created a stressful environment at home, as Katie was busy driving Cayden to his therapies everyday and not being able to have a career of her own.

Jared tried to help her out as much as possible, but he had the mindset that the military took care of the medical bills for the last ten years, so he should be giving his all back to the military. There are many that thought he had already given enough.

"Hun, I understand you want to travel and visit these places, but we can't afford it right now," Jared spoke softly.

She had been asking to travel to Paris multiple times in the last three years.

"What happens if there is an emergency and we can't afford to survive? We are still recovering from the Disney World trip we took two years ago."

Jared and Katie had been talking for months about taking trips and going somewhere with just the two of them. They normally spend their vacations in Tennessee and try to spend missed time with family as much as possible. However, they had never taken a vacation by themselves, with no children, ever. Katie needed a break, she deserved one, but Jared could never accept the amount of money and danger international vacations consisted of. Katie, however, was relentless.

"Jared, I am serious," Katie said, "I am ready for a break. As much as I hate to say something like that, I just need a few days of us. No therapies, no meltdowns, no duties. Just you and me relaxing. You know how bad I have always wanted to travel and France would be a dream come true."

"I know hun," said Jared. "We will. We just need to save up the extra income for a four wheel drive vehicle for the winter. You of all people know how bad winters can get in Tennessee and I want to make sure if a storm comes, I can still get to work or travel on the road if need be."

"We have enough money saved up for five vehicles," exclaimed Kaite! "I want to go to Paris with you by my side. Let's take the kids to mom and fly out there for a week and relax. You are leaving for Iraq again next year, so we need some time to ourselves. This time we need to do something special, something just for us!"

Like always, she was right. Jared could lead hundreds of Marines in battle, make hair splitting decisions in an instant, but never outsmart his own wife. She had given up so much for this family and he often forgets that. He knew what had to be done, he just didn't want to.

He had this everlasting fear that something could happen if they traveled to a place like Paris. All he could think about was the attacks in November of 2015. He could never live with himself if something happened to Katie on his watch. However, there was no way he could continue to hold her off with that mindset. In all reality, what was the chance that something like that would happen with their visit, at the exact moment they were there, at the exact time they were visiting. Time for Jared to put his wife first, and the job second.

"You know what, fine Kate, it's a done deal. Set it up with your parents and let's go get your passport first thing in the morning. No questions asked, let's do it. We can have a passport ordered tomorrow and whatever date they say it will arrive, we will plan to leave that week. We could all use a break," Jared stated.

"Really!"

She was excited and it made Jared happy. She was right, he would be deploying for the sixth time within the year and pre-deployment training would be picking up before they knew it. A seven month deployment easily turned into a year with workups. Cayden has just started being homeschooled due to the public school system and he knew of all of the deployments, she would be the busiest on this one.

"Yep, we are doing this. Nothing is going to stop us from hitting up Paris," said Jared as he walked towards the calendar. He wrote *Passport* on the calendar. "See, done deal," he stated.

As he turned around to face Katie, she threw herself in his arms. He hadn't seen her this happy in years, as she was always so tired. For the first time in a long time, it even made Jared happy too. He smiled from ear to ear. Deep down inside though, he knew that things never go as planned, or as anticipated. He can put on a confident and happy face all day for his wife, but in the back of his head he would always have concern over their safety

CHAPTER FOUR

The Meeting

<u>*August 12th 2019*</u>

The smell from the sheet over his head was musty and the dampness from his breath was beginning to increase. They had been driving for over an hour, but from the constant left turns they made, he assumed they were making several loops to throw him off of their route.

It was a well known aspect within the Task Force that the Army of Islam had a main bivouac close to the American encampment. However, the current stance taken from the top leaders was to monitor closely, instead of taking decisive action. This gave him great confidence that an airstrike on the organizations particular location was likely not going to happen.

The noise from the outside was particularly loud, surely due to his sight being taken from having the sheet over his head. He could hear what he deemed to be farm animals, probably for feeding the group. Jared also heard kids shouting and playing, maybe a group of children outside a school. He couldn't recall any marked educational buildings in the area from his map study, but that didn't make the assumption untrue. The maps were hardly kept up to date, which got them in trouble often. Suddenly, he heard what appeared to be the opening of a metal gate, as if someone outside was letting them in.

They had slowed down almost to a stop, so this had to be it. They lurched forward from slowing down and began a right hand turn that had to be in a compound. The vehicle stopped with a slide and the doors to the vehicle began to open.

He felt someone grab his left arm under his armpit and pull him out of the vehicle. What was interesting to Jared was that they were not being overly aggressive. Instead of throwing him out of the vehicle onto the ground and kicking him around, they instead pulled him out like a police officer removing someone from the back seat. They wanted him out of the vehicle, but didn't want his head to get banged up on the way out.

Someone was pulling him to the left. Instead of being rushed and jabbed to lurch forward, he instead was being directed somewhere. He heard another door open and a gentle push from behind to make him aware that they wanted him to go somewhere. Suddenly, the sheet from around his face was removed. As he regained his vision, his hands were unbound.

The door slammed shut behind him, he was suddenly alone. As his eyes adjusted, he could see that he was in a small room, with a cot. On the cot there was a military issued liner with a small pillow. They had obviously taken the liners from a convoy they had hit and used them for their own people.

Looking around the room, he had the bare necessities to live with. There was a large metal bin which looked to be halfway through the floor. A white PVC pipe was snuggly fitted through the wall that appeared to have a slow stream of water going into the metal bin. There was probably a small drain hole under the floor that prevented the bin from overflowing.

In one of the corners, there was a wooden box and a large roll of military waste kit wag bags, his given method to use the bathroom. Other than three main items of bed, water, and bathroom, there was a small wooden shelf against the wall with nothing on it. Jared had a means to survive, although not ideal.

The door was a metal standard issue cell door, with a sliding hole at the bottom of the door. Just enough to slide a plate under, but not a person's foot. There was enough room to do a set of jumping jacks next to the cot, nothing more.

Jared sat down on the cot and began to collect his thoughts. Why had they not thrown him around like a prisoner, or at least beaten him? He had expected to be put through the ringer before anyone would trust him, but this was an entirely different side he hadn't expected.

He mentally accepted his fate, as it could have resulted in a much worse fashion. At least he isn't bruised and beaten, other than the cut on his head from the previous encounter when the man hit Jared with the rifle. Although he didn't think he would be able to, Jared was determined to try and get some rest. As he laid his head down on the small pillow, his thoughts immediately drifted off to Katie.

The loud screech of the sliding plate on the bottom of the door made Jared jolt open his eyes. He immediately sat up and waited for what was about to happen, nervously expecting anything. Jared watched as a plate of food slid under the door and the metal plate was pulled back shut quickly..

Jared stood up and said softly, "Thank you for the food."

He received no response, but he still believed that being kind would result in better treatment and maybe a sliver of respect. The food consisted of some sort of meat, a tortilla and some rice. Two bottles of water was also rolled behind the food and he immediately twisted the lid off of one of them and chugged the entire bottle. He hadn't realized how desiccated he felt and he wanted to make sure that dehydration wouldn't be his worst enemy.

The food looked good, though he wasn't quite sure if he should risk eating it. He would never earn their trust if he didn't show trust towards them though, so he began to eat. As he was eating, he attempted to listen to the outside noises. He could not hear much, so he assumed that he was more alone than not. Before Jared knew it, the entire plate of food was gone. He gently pushed the plate back towards the door, trying to make the retrieval of the dish easier for his captor.

Jared began to check his pockets for anything that he may have carried with him. Other than some lint, he had a can of Grizzly Wintergreen chewing tobacco and a few pogs$_1$ that was used on the camp as replacement money for real coins. He had something he needed to do, as he didn't know if his memory would fail him. As he looked around, he tried to find a simple solution that he could come back to down the road if need be. He wanted to join this organization, but he realized that he was still an American and they were not going to just trust him right off the bat because he said he switching sides.

Jared picked up the liner and looked at the cot. As he turned over the bed and looked on the underside of it, he had an idea. The entire floor was full of small pebbles and he would use them in the same notion as ranger beads. He began to pick them up and went to the corner of the room. He put one of the larger pebbles he had found against the center of one of the walls, this would mark his start location.

Jared skipped the first corner after marking his starting point, then moved to the next corner moving clockwise. In this corner he placed nine pebbles, two pebbles in the next and three small pebbles in the fourth and last corner. This would work, as nobody probably ever came here to clean the room. If they do, then oh well, Jared just needed not to forget.

He was pleased with his method and sat back down. Not knowing what time of day it was threw him off of calibration. He felt as though he needed to go back to sleep, likely due to the lack of nutrition in his body. He had to be careful not to burn too many calories until he could determine his daily intake. Jared laid back down and tried to go back to sleep. As anticipated, the sleep didn't come.

♦

Eventually Jared could hear footsteps coming down the short hallway. The sound was intriguing though, as footsteps wasn't really the correct term. He heard a hard step and then a sliding knock sound. He needed to be ready for anything. This could be someone carrying something heavy like a large piece of lumber, a large hammer, anything. He sat up slowly and waited for whatever was to come. He heard the manipulation of the lock on the door and it began to slide open. Jared tensed his body and prepared for a fight.

In the doorway stood a man in the shadows. He was slightly hunched to one side and had a well groomed black beard. The sound he had heard, was the prosthetic leg this man had. No, Jared was wrong, it was more of a wooden plank used as a leg on his right side. From the looks of the way the man stood, the wooden contraption was more of a crutch used under his armpit that the man leaned on to walk with. What was even more interesting was what the man was wearing.

Covering the top of his head was a black turban, with no markings or designs. Plain black, with the perfect tightness fitting to his head. It looked as though it belonged there permanently. With Jared's eyes adjusting from the light from the open door, he realized that the man is wearing an Army Combat Uniform Jacket with no markings. Under the ACU he is wearing a thawb, which is an ankle length garment that has long sleeves and resembles a tunic. Also black in color, the man looks impressive even with the one leg.

"How are you being treated," the man asks Jared immediately?

His voiced portrayed genuine concern. However, Jared knew he must choose his words wisely and not fall for any deception that the man has planned.

"I am doing well, I have no complaints," Jared states.

"Your Arabic is good, I am genuinely surprised!"

"Thank you," Jared exclaims.

As Jared watched the mans face, he comes to the conclusion that the man just wants to have a conversation, so Jared eases himself as much as possible and prepares to examine and interpret every word the man says.

From behind the man comes a young child, around the age of twelve or thirteen. He is pulling a chair behind him and sets it down inside the room. Without a word, the child leaves and scurries away down the hallway. The man slowly sets the wooden crutch to the side and settles himself down into the chair. The conversation is about to start and Jared needs to be on his best game in order to capitalize off of this encounter. He may not get another chance if he screws this up.

The man starts, "My name is Abu Bakr al-Adir, but you can call me Adir. I was sent here to have an initial conversation with you. The elders are interested in how you have ended up in your current situation?"

Jared needs to be careful while making his intentions known early on.

"Hello Adir, it is a pleasure to meet you. My name is Jared Sterling, but feel free to call me Jared."

Jared gives a fake last name, he by no means wants the organization to search for and locate his family.

"In regards to my current situation, what exactly do you mean?" Jared asks, trying to see what kind of information Adir will give him.

Unfortunately, Jared is still concerned about his overall endstate. Who is to say that once this conversation ends, Adir will not give the signal to have his men come in the room and kill him. In order to feel the situation out, Jared must see how careful Adir is and how much information he is willing to give him. He knows that if Adir begins to lay out intimate plans and high level secrets, the outcome of Jared's survival is not likely.

"Jared," Adir starts, "why ask a question you already know the answer to? I will entertain such a question this one time, but from here on, I will not condone any sort of game to be played. Why are you here? Why have you ended up in this room, sitting in front of me?"

Adir had a new look on his face, one of deep thoughts, but with a serious look that might have sparked a small ounce of fear within Jared. He had to make his move and ensure Adir knew he was serious.

"I have no intentions of playing games. I am here for one reason, I am tired of the fighting. I am going to be up front with you Adir. I have personally been fighting against your organization, your people, for quite some time now. From all of this fighting, I have learned one thing, I am tired. I am tired of fighting against you for something I don't believe in. Fighting for people I can't stand people who are only making decisions because they are stuck in their current situation."

"Leaders who are calling the shots because if they make the right calls and have beneficial results, they can advance and gain higher positions of power back in the states. I am tired of fighting against people who are fighting for survival, for their home, for their beliefs. Months ago I came to the realization that I may be on the wrong side, or quite possibly I am fighting a losing battle."

Adir shifted his weight in his chair and gave a long glaring stare that seemed to penetrate Jared's soul. He asked very slowly and clearly to Jared.

"Jared, what exactly are you telling me? Before you answer, I want you to be very careful how you choose your next words as the repercussions from them could be everlasting."

Jared glared right back at Adir, as if the statement was a mockery of his intentions.

"Adir, my friend. The answer to why I am here is easy. I wish to join the Army of Islam and help you defeat the American infidels!"

CHAPTER FIVE

The Blast

Jared had been sitting in the chair Adir left behind for several hours now, with no hints of where the conversation he previously had with Adir would lead. He half expected Adir to open the door and let Jared walk out, getting straight to work, but of course that would never happen.

Suddenly, the door smashed open and a group of five men with AK's rushed into the room. All five were screaming and pointing their weapons at Jared's body. He must have made a mistake, obviously not playing his cards right. They were going to kill him right here, no questions asked, not even give him a chance.

One of the men kicked the chair's leg out, causing it to break and forcing Jared on his feet. A second person grabbed the chair and threw it against the wall. A third member walked behind Jared and jabbed the muzzle of his weapon in the middle of Jared's back. Sharp pain forced him to step forward, fighting to stay on his feet. Jared walked forward, trying to comply as much as he possibly could.

The five men escorting Jared had a formation that ensured he did as they instructed. One man behind him, ready to smash the barrel of his weapon in Jared's back, something he was not shy about. Jared feared his spine would break with only a few more impacts. The second and third men were to his side, both with their weapons pointed straight at Jared's face. The last two, number four and five, were directly in front of Jared walking backwards. Both had their AK-47's pointed at Jared's body as well, making a total of five rifles all pointing directly at Jared. He hoped none had a negligent discharge, not that it would matter to anyone else.

He realized that he was in a building that was not quite tall, but modernized. This was not the small underground shack he had imagined from his dark room below. There was a set of stairs in front of them and it was apparent they were to start climbing. They eventually made it up to the second floor and went to a window that was facing the city. They were in a long room with windows covering the entire east side, spaced about four feet in between each other. There had been discussions about recent structures being built in Ramadi and this appeared to be one of them.

One of the biggest conversations that took place back at their camp was defending newly structured buildings being funded by the government, with obvious objections from The Army of Islam. Now Jared stood in one, inhabited by the organization that opposed its creation. Up ahead stood Adir, looking out one of the windows. Without his wooden crutch, he appeared taller, more confident. Jared knew he had to have a prosthetic leg on.

"Hello Jared, how was your rest," he asked, without looking in his direction?

"Fine Adir, thank you. What do I owe the pleasure of seeing you again on such a short notice?"

Jared wanted to appear confident and show that he had no fear living with his adversaries. He looked out of the window to see what Adir was staring at.

"Well Jared, you mentioned that you wanted to join our organization. You said you would fight for our beliefs, defeat those that are against us in the field of battle. Am I right?"

Adir paused after the question.

" I have decided to give you a choice based on your words. I am going to offer you a chance to prove yourself. Are you are willing to make those words you spoke real actions, or otherwise prove you are lying to me which of course will result in one thing."

Adir slowly looked to the right and peered in Jared's eyes. Then slowly Adir turned back to looking out of the window.

"The building we are currently standing in is a commercial structure built to form and house the local government officials. The Americans have helped the creation of this building and continue to drive around it. You want to keep a close eye on the structure until the local government can defend themselves."

"What the Americans do not know, is that we, the Army of Islam, are the local government. The Army of Islam has had control over the local officials since the very beginning. There are no chances, no mistakes made, no quick decisions within the Army. We are calculated, we maintain control over everything we wish to have control over."

"Welcome to what we here in the organization like to call 3-Story Jared. This building is the main control point for the region, which we will prove shortly."

Adir began to walk from the window, turned around and reached for a device on a table behind them. The device looked similar to what a claymore firing device would resemble. There were no wires connected to the object, but what appeared to be a small light bulb on the top and a handle to squeeze on the side.

"Now on to your choice, the action of you doing one thing or another. In four minutes and twenty seconds, an American convoy of five military grade vehicles will be driving down that road, from the East. They must slow down to go around that small curve in the road. When they do, they will be surveying this building to see if there is anything suspicious."

"However, we have had people here every single day for the last two months and not once have they ever stopped. You see we understand that they do not wish to be here any more than we want you to be. Why should they risk their lives for a building that will not benefit them, when they can slowly drive by and report that everything is all clear. Today, that will not be the case."

Adir once again turned towards Jared, this time extending his hand slowly in Jared's direction. Jared knew immediately what was about to happen and he needed to make a decision rather quickly. Was he ready to take this leap, ready to make this statement to the entire world. There would be no turning back at this point.

"Jared my friend, you now have two minutes and ten seconds to make a choice. Choice one, you take this device from my hand and squeeze the lever to the closed position. This will initiate the signal that activates the Improvised Explosive Device below that is buried in the road along the small curve. It will then be set to initiate and explode once the first vehicle breaks the line of sight from the infared that is currently between the two signs below."

Jared looked down at the road to see what Adir was speaking about. He could not see any sign of a buried device, nor could he see anybody watching the suspected area. He did, however, see the two signs that Adir spoke of, but obviously could not see any infrared lights or lasers from his position. This could be a test and even if Jared set the device, nothing could happen. If Adir was smart, then he wouldn't want to set off an explosion near his own position, as this could initiate a counter attack. Jared had less than a minute to decide.

"Fifty seconds Jared, what are you going to do? Are you ready to take that leap you spoke of? All you have to do is set the device, show your true intentions," Adir challenged Jared!

Jared was sweating, he had to make a choice. Would the IED even go off? Could there be one planted where Adir says there is? There was only one way to find out and Jared had made his choice. He had been through nineteen of his own explosions while riding in the Mine Resistant Ambush Protected vehicles. Although not a fun ride, he had survived. At the same time, there were some that had not.

Jared turned to look at Adir, staring right into his eyes.

"I don't understand why you would question my integrity, question my loyalty to the cause I had proclaimed to you while looking you in the eyes!"

Jared reached his right hand out to Adir slowly, handing him the device. As Adir look down at the mechanism, a smile crept along his face. The light on top of the handle was green. Jared slowly turned around and went to the window to watch the oncoming convoy. Suddenly, he saw the front end of the first vehicle coming from the far east, heading towards the small curve in the road. As the rest of the convoy began to come into view, Jared stared at the curve, waiting for the explosion, if any. He still had his doubts.

The first vehicle began to slow down, preparing itself for the curve, for the possibility of an explosion that may come from a hazard in the road. The Army of Islam was well known for using these typical locations for attacks on American convoys. Without warning, the vehicle came to an abrupt stop, they must have seen something that made them cautious.

SGT HAYES

Sergeant Hayes was an experienced Mobile Assault Marine. Through many deployments as a machine gunner, he had spent his entire combat career inside of a Humvee or in a turret. He had experience, no doubt about it, but the fear of losing a Marine kept him awake most nights. As he sat here at in the middle of the road, he had that strange feeling that came over him that he had felt many times before. Now that he was in charge, he couldn't lead and protect the Marines over a feeling though.

"All vics, halt" Hayes barked over the radio!

He needed to see what was going on up ahead. He hated blind spots in the road and this was definitely one of them. The problem was that he couldn't see crap from inside the front seat. He missed being a gunner in the turret. You could see for days and when it was time to party, he was always the first one to put rounds down range. Time to let the young guys get some too. Nowadays the gunners sat in the back seat and controlled a remote system mounted on top of the vehicle. Even though the gunner was inside, he could still see better when controlling the camera system.

"Parker, scan up ahead. Check out that corner and see if you can see anything strange," he yelled back to the gunner.

JARED

After a few minutes of the convoy being stopped, Jared seen the turret on the first truck begin to move left and right. They were scanning for something, trying to locate what was making them so suspicious. The first vehicle had a M2HB mounted on a R400S-Mk2, a 3-axis stabilized remote weapon station weighing less than 880 pounds.

This allowed the Marine to control the turret and weapon system from inside the vehicle. It was much safer than when Jared was a Machine gunner in Ramadi in 2006, but also reduced the visibility a turret gunner had in Jared's opinion.

The weapon system eventually went back to the front, they were making their decision within the vehicle. Jared had been in that situation so many times, eventually they all blend together. The patrol leader would either say to turn around, sit in place and call the Explosive Ordnance Disposal Team[4], or push through and hope it was nothing.

This was a lot of pressure to rest on a young man's shoulders, that leader had the option of saving lives, or losing them. No one blamed them, nor did they envy them. There came a point where Marines in that position just wanted someone else to make the calls that day to let their minds settle for emptiness just one time.

The choice was made, the first vehicle lurched forward slowly, it was obvious their decision was to push on and hope for the best. Jared watched from a distance, yearning to know their fate. He had never expected for this day to come so quickly, but he had his own mission to do. If there was a bomb planted in the road, there was nothing he could do about it now. Deep down inside, he was still hopeful that one didn't exist though. Hope didn't do much these days anymore.

SGT HAYES

Sergeant Hayes had made his choice, they were pushing through. They had been through this area a hundred times, each time going smooth. The only difference was that feeling. He couldn't tell what caused it, but without any validation he had to keep going. It was probably nothing and the men were ready to get back to camp and eat some chow.

As Hayes settled back in his seat, ready to push on, everything went black!

JARED

Suddenly, smoke and dirt exploded into the air, followed immediately by a large booming sound. A tire could be seen tumbling through the air from the driver side of the vehicle, out running the smoke cloud. As the smoke began to settle, Jared could see the destruction on the vehicle, the front end destroyed. The other four trucks quickly came forward and created a defensive perimeter around the first truck, about fifty meters away.

Marines were jumping out of the vehicle, conducting their five and twenty five meter checks. The idea was to look out their windows for the immediate five meters surrounding their vehicle. This was so they wouldn't jump out of their truck and step on a device right away. Once they safely excited their vehicle, they would check the twenty five meters around their vehicle to ensure its safety. After completing that step, they would start their V-Sweep to the downed vehicle.

The V-Sweep is a highly effective technique for dismounted investigation of danger areas. The system needed to be done carefully and slowly. They use handheld minesweepers to check the ground, but they didn't always work. Everything they did was on hopes and prayers, always assuming the next step would be the last.

Within minutes, three Marines were up to the destroyed truck to check on their brothers. Jared watched the first truck and began to count as young men stepped out. One, two, and three. That was all he had seen so far. Three people had stepped out of the first truck and began to walk around and go sit on the edge of the street while the others stood security. Jared continued to watch the driver side front door and waiting to see if he saw any movement. He saw none!

SGT HAYES

"Daniels, wake up," shouted Sergeant Hayes.

The blast had come out of nowhere, he still was having a hard time breathing. The amount of smoke and dust that flies through the air when an IED goes off is impossible to describe, it just takes over the air. Nothing but darkness, nothing but fear.

So far everyone was ok, except for Daniels, the driver. He was still slumped over in his seat, not responding to Hayes' shouts.

The driver side door was crumbled, no way for Daniels to escape if he did wake up. Maybe he wasn't going to, if the door looked like that, what did Daniels look li….

Hayes stopped, he couldn't think like that, he had to lead the Marines. The team leaders were doing their job and setting security. Hayes had to ensure his driver was going to be okay. Sergeant Hayes climbed into the back seat and started to crawl towards the front of the vehicle towards Daniels.

"Daniels, bro, I am coming for you. Everything is going to be okay. I am coming to get you man."

JARED

"Well done, you have proven your intentions are sincere. I didn't think you had it in you. It can be quite easy to say one thing, but to actual put the people you used to live with in direct harm, that shows something. This does not mean you are part of this organization, or you can claim allegiance to the Army of Islam, it only means you are speaking the truth and your actions speak clearly. I will be sure to explain this to the leader when I meet with him again. Do you understand," Adir asked?

"I understand Adir, thank you," Jared replied softly. "May I return to my room now," he asked Adir?

Movement, Jared sees the driver climbing out of the rear driver side door with another Marine, his must have been inoperable from the blast.

"I believe the damage is done here," Jared spoke as he turned from the window and faced Adir.

"I am intrigued to see what our next visit will consist of."

Adir nodded to the five men that brought Jared up the stairs from his room earlier. Only three of them began to direct him back to the bottom floor. As Jared turned away from Adir, he felt Adir's hand grab his arm.

"Tomorrow we will have a conversation about what you can offer us here at the Army of Islam and why we should consider your request," stated Adir.

Jared nodded and began to walk down the stairs and head back to his room. He was still fighting with everything he had to hold back the tears.

<u>CHAPTER SIX</u>

The COC

<u>*August 14th 2019*</u>

The Combat Operations Center₃ (COC) at Camp Elmore had just received a radio transmission about a convoy that had hit an IED. The radio watch on duty immediately started scribbling as many notes as he could in order to transcribe the controlled chaos that was coming over the radio.

The Watch Chief stood up and walked over closer to the radio and listened in. He had already sent a runner to get the Watch Officer in case the situation developed even more and presented worse conditions. It wasn't too often that attacks occurred in this area any more, but the threat was always there.

"Lance Corporal Banks, let me know if you need assistance getting notes and handling the other units that are out in the Area of Operations," stated the Watch Chief.

"Aye Aye Staff Sergeant," the radio operator quickly shouted back.

Staff Sergeant Hunter knew from experience to leave the young warrior alone. He had been in the Marine's position many years ago and knew all he wanted was to be left alone so he could do his job the best he could. The Lance Corporal had friends out there and he was going to do whatever it took to accomplish the mission in front of him.

The radio squelched back alive and reports started to flow in. The voice was from Sergeant Hayes, the patrol leader from Three Bravo.

{Line 1 - Time Now}
{Line 2 - Three Bravo Grid 47384 - 87437}
{Line 3 - Three Bravo Actual}

Break

{Line 4 - Placed / One-Five-Five Shell}

{Line 5 - No}

{Line 6 - Vic one disabled / No casualties}

Break

{Line 7 - Mission ended}

{Line 8 - Three Sixty Defense}

{Line 9 - Routine}

It was confirmed, Three Bravo had hit an IED while on a mounted patrol driving down 20th street. So far no casualties were reported, but that could change in an instant. Staff Sergeant Hunter was still waiting on the Watch Officer to show up and anticipated the aggravation that was sure to come. Gunnery Sergeant Jared Tremble had disappeared the night before and rumors were already spreading.

The rumor mill of junior Marines, notoriously known as the Lance Corporal Underground, had two scenarios floating around the camp. One side said he had been grabbed walking near the perimeter late at night, something he was well known for doing on his own. The other side whispers that he willingly left the camp to join a terrorist organization.

The underground came to this conclusion as a number of Marines recall seeing the Gunnery Sergeant getting into an argument with the Company First Sergeant. They also know this happened on the same night of his disappearance. Some found this as an intentional distraction. Typically though, the Lance Corporal undergrounds rumors were far fetched and seldom resembles any accuracy. One can't help but wonder though.

"Staff Sergeant, what do we got?"

The Watch Officer suddenly appeared at the entrance, the runner had found him.

"Well Sir, it appears that Three Bravo hit an IED on 20th street, near the new building that got assembled for the government restructure."

"Any casualties," the Watch Officer asked?

"None reported at this time," Hunter replied.

"Sounds good, keep me updated. For some reason, higher leadership wants constant updates from within the AO as of this morning. It's unusual, but they have us reporting straight to Division, by-passing the Battalion and Regiment!"

"Understood Sir, when I hear something I'll send a runner your way," Hunter responded.

This must have something to do with Gunny Tremble, they never reported straight to Division on matters regarding IED strikes or small arms fire. Hunter decided to watch his step and ensure he crossed all his t's and dotted all his i's. Tremble was his good friend, so he was interested to know what was going on, but he also had a duty to protect his Marines and ensure nothing from Division put them at an unruly risk. Time will tell, until then, it was time to stay alert!

♦

As Jared sat in his room, he continued to picture the explosion, trying to decide if he had done the right thing. He knew this was going to be hard, but he didn't think it would all happen so fast. He had planned out everything so much in his head, he forgot to consider the emotional aspect of it all. He would literally be fighting against his own family. People he had known for so many years, fought side by side with through many battles. They had been through so much together.

Enough was enough though, something had to be done. Not to mention no one had come to his side when he went through the worst time of his life. When he was at the lowest point he had ever imagined, nobody came to pick him up. None of them can understand what he is going through. How could they, they were all too worried about careers, or houses, or their cars. Nothing that was really important. Not about their own family, or his. They couldn't even imagine the idea of losing....

"Are you awake, Sir?"

A voice suddenly shook him out of the haze he was drifting off too, thinking about his actions. He didn't recognize the voice, but how could he so early in the game?

"Yes, I am, may I ask who you are," Jared responded?

No response, how odd. Could Jared be hearing things, hallucinating people speaking to him? It had only been two days, how could he be suffering from being here so soon? Were there others here, being held against their will as well?

Moments later he heard footsteps walking on the cement floor outside. The pace was not fast, more like a roving guard. Like someone was sent down here to check on him. It was the first time he had noticed the sound, but the last few days that was the last thing on his mind. You never know how your body and its senses will deal with a situation like this. Within minutes, the sound was gone along with whatever person was sent down here to check on their prisoner.

"Yes, I am here," came the voice again, a low whisper.

Jared was right, there was someone down here with him. By the sound of his voice, it appeared the other man was in the room next to him.

"Hello, I can hear you. My name is Jared, what can I call you," he asked the voice?

"You can call me Bashar," he replied.

"Nice to meet you Bashar, are you a prisoner here," Jared asked?

"I am, I have been for many years now. I never leave this room, unless needed by the organization for certain things."

"If you don't mind me asking, why have you been down here all this time," asked Jared?

"No, I do not mind you asking," replied Bashar. "It happens to be a long story, but from what I have heard from the last few days, you have the time to hear it. Seven years ago, I used to work as a Muzari. More specifically, I was a poppy farmer, one that happened to be doing quite well at his occupation. You see, it is hard to have an opium poppy farm within this country, when the Americans continue to despise that way of life and destroy your crops. No matter what I would do, they would continue to either burn down my crops, or have the local army destroy them."

"At the same time though, Abu Bakr al-Adir was heavily invested in helping me with the farm. I was able to pay him and the organization forty percent of all profits, in return they would provide protection. They were able to keep the Americans away, lead them in other directions when the Americans came close to my farm."

Bashar took a break, it appeared he stopped to see if anyone was listening, or coming back down the hallway.

"However, Adir became more aggravated with our deal, quickly demanding more money, a better negotiation for him. I was not able to come to an agreement, because I was already providing so much of the profit to him, I could barely give anything to my own family after paying for the farm itself. That's when the local armies suddenly became interested in my farm, likely due to Adir telling them to do so."

"At first it was my small plots, the easy to burn now and threaten to come back later type of conversation. My farm has been in my family for many years, passed from generation to generation. It was a way to survive, provide for our family. We never hurt anyone, or despised others beliefs. We believed in our faith, grew our crops and tried to ensure that we would survive through the year. No one ever bothered us until the local army came and attempted to force us to shut down. They continued to harass my family and destroy our way of life."

Bashar took a deep breath and continued on.

"Then one day, the local police chief found my main farm. The large plot of land that had my main crop growing. The one that provided the largest part of my income. Typically, they arrived angry and shouting, not wanting to hear anything I had to say. At that time, I had Abu Bakr al-Adir's thirteen year old son working for me in the field."

"It was Adir's way of forcing his young son to learn what hard work was and not have things given to you because of your name. When the police arrived, they immediately lit the crops on fire by pouring gasoline throughout the entire field. In the middle of the field was a small shack that we stored tools in. Adir's son had decided to hide in there.

Quickly, the Americans showed up to provide

THE AMERICAN TERRORIST

assistance. They had seen the black smoke from the road and came over immediately. Adir's boy still remained in the small shed though since he was scared and didn't know what to do."

Bashar began to sob slightly, obviously upset from what he was about to tell Jared.

"Once the fire was lit, there was no escaping that shack. He was surrounded by flames and I tried to run over and tell the soldiers. The Americans tried to help me, but it was too late. Within minutes the tool shed was on fire and Adir's boy died a horrible death, all alone and afraid. The police chief and his men left as quickly as they came and didn't even attempt to help me with the boy."

"I walked out to the building and recovered what was left of the Adir's sons body and brought the remains back to Adir. He blamed me and punished me with diya, or what is known as blood money. This is the standard punishment for an unintentional murder of someones family and since I didn't have any money to pay him, I was thrown in here seven years ago. His son would be twenty and to this day I am still being punished for something done by our own people."

"The Police Chief didn't get off as easy. Adir had members of the Army of Islam collect him and his entire family. At first, they forced him to watch his entire family burned alive, right in the middle of the village. Once they were gone, Adir himself lit the Police Chief on fire and stood over him as he screamed. They say he didn't flinch, didn't move, nothing. He was cold as steel while delivering his punishment."

Jared was shocked by the story and could not get a good read on the Bashar since he could not see his face. His voice seemed genuine enough, but Jared just could not tell. He could be fabricating the story to gain Jared's allegiance, or he could not.

"Bashar, I am truly sorry to hear this story. I cannot express the sorrow I have for you and your family. The police unit in charge during that time should have to pay for what they have done to you."

Jared paused one last time and decided to go ahead and tell Bashar. It was likely Bashar would stay here until he was dead anyway, so why not give him just a little reassurance.

Jared continued on, "As a matter of fact, this is why I am here. I am joining the organization and becoming a true follower of The Army of Islam to fight what is wrong with this world. I have fought against you and your people for so many years for nothing, realizing that I was fighting for the wrong cause. I will not anymore, I refuse to! It's people like you being forced to suffer because of the ignorance and incompetence leadership leading the armies in countries like this one."

Jared was getting heated up and could feel the anger swell up inside of him. He had to calm down before he went to far and told Bashar too much.

"Bashar, my friend, if you need anything from

me, please let me know. If there is anything I can do to ease your pain or provide you with a sense of relief, do not hesitate to ask. I am sickened by your story and will do whatever is in my power to make any soldier like the ones that treated you so unfairly, with the harshest punishment I can deliver. This I promise you."

Jared was done now, as he turned around and walked back to his cot. He had wondered how truthful Bashar had been with him. He had only just talked to Jared this one time and shared his entire story right away. Jared was always like this though, he never trusted anyone or anything.

He couldn't stand the people that read an article on social media and took it as gospel. It was like people didn't know that anyone could write a story online and share it with the world. Just because one person said that you can catch cancer by passing gas in a swimming pool doesn't make it true. It drove Jared crazy what society has come to.

Jared was a man of facts, needed to conduct research and scan peer-reviewed journals to pass judgement on something. In regards to Bashar, there wasn't much he could do but wait and decide if he could trust this man or not. If Bashar was telling the truth, he could be a good ally. He probably didn't get many visitors down here and longed for a companion to have a conversation with. Only time will tell and Jared had to be careful. If he gets caught up in the underground drama, then his entire plan could fail. He won't let that happen, couldn't, he had to much inside of him to let it fail.

As Jared got ready to lay down on his cot, he looked around his room. As he stretched his sore muscles, he looked at the four corners of his room. As he slowly turned three hundred and sixty degrees, he counted slowly in his head. He wouldn't forget, he had too much riding on it. Finally he laid down and tried to fall asleep. He spent the remaining moments awake repeating the numbers in his head. Zero, nine, two, three. Zero, nine, two, three.

CHAPTER SEVEN

The Plot

August 16th 2019

Abu Bakr al-Adir had been awake since four in the morning, as the first prayer time today was at 4:11. Once he got up, there was no going back to bed for him, he had too much to do. Without him, the entire organization would fail, something he could not let happen. He needed the Army of Islam and wouldn't let anyone take it away from him.

After his prayers, Adir sat down to drink some coffee made from arabica beans and think about his son, Amad. Adir missed him so much and could never diminish the hatred in his heart for what had happened to him. He would fight and kill as many Americans as he could to honor his son and to seek revenge for their actions.

This happened to be one of the reasons he had yet to trust Jared and why there was still

92

questions in his mind on whether to kill him or not. On one side of the spectrum, having a rogue American soldier willing to join his organization and share secrets with them could be a blessing. On the other hand, Jared could be a spy and be trying to bring down the entire organization from the inside out. He had told himself that he would never trust any American, but could that be the wrong choice at this moment?

One of Adir's greatest warriors and defenders, Asim, limped through the door suddenly. Asim had been by Adir's side since the beginning, always willing to get his hands dirty and bloody for Adir. Last year, Asim had been shot in the back of his right leg, smashing through his knee. Ever since then, Asim had been more of an advisor instead of a warrior.

"Good Morning Sheikh, I was told you wanted to see me first thing this morning," Asim stated using the common title they used for Adir.

"Yes Asim, I did," replied Adir.

"What is it that I can do for you Sheikh?"

"I wish to receive your council on the American, Jared"

"Ahh, I see. May I sit," Asim asked?

"Of course, you are like a brother to me. You have fought with me through every battle. Helped me bury Amad, even mourned with me. You are always welcome by my side."

"Thank you for your kind words," replied Asim. "What type of council are you looking for?"

"What do you think about the American? Do we trust him, should we kill him? Do we need more time and hear what else he has to say? I am very torn about this entire ordeal. I am not sure if I should be trusting my soul, or sticking to the laws."

"Well Sheikh, I think this is a very trying time and we need to be smart about the decision we make here. For instance, if the American is telling the truth and truly wants to join our cause, he could be a very valuable asset. The amount of knowledge, plans and detailed information he could give us would shape the entire future of the Army," stated Asim.

"However, if that isn't the case and he isn't being entirely truthful to us, then we could potentially be setting ourselves up for the greatest defeat ever. This is a difficult position to be in, with a very challenging decision ahead of you. At this point, my council would be to wait and gather more information before making a decision. He can do us no harm by staying below in the holding room. We can continue to escort him, bring him to the interrogation room if we need to speak to him. Not to mention, we also have one other tool we could use."

"What tool would that be Asim," asked Adir? "Bashar!"

Adir had forgotten about Bashar many years ago. He had made it a point to throw the traitor down in the holding rooms and forget he ever existed. Adir missed his son so much, it still hurt so much at night when it was time to go to sleep. Everytime he closed his eyes, he could see his sons face looking back at him.

However, everytime he attempted to adore his boys face, it quickly faded to the burnt and empty face that they had buried in the ground. The anger he felt for Bashar quickly rose, coming from deep within his body. It hurt so bad that it made him shake. He closed his eyes as he spoke to Asim.

"That is true, that traitor is down there still. I forgot he was still alive," replied Adir angrily.

"We could make him a couple promises, show him a light at the end of the tunnel and see what kind of information he can extract from Jared. The American may say a little more to someone he believes is incarcerated forever and has no ability to share the information he is given. This could be a great asset for us to use."

"Then what, we would let him go," demanded Adir.

"We can do whatever we like, say whatever we want, make Bashar believe whatever we want him to believe," Asim spoke softly.

Adir stared at Asim for a moment, with deep anger and hurtful eyes. As bad as he wanted to refuse this council, he knew he would be foolish to do so. He stood up to walk away, as he was turning his back, he paused for just a moment.

"Do whatever it is you need to do brother."

Asim was right, as always.

♦

A door slammed, followed by a group of footsteps rushing towards the door. There was no time to prepare his body, only close his eyes and try his best not to fight what was about to happen. Even if he wanted to, he couldn't defend himself against one of them from the years of sitting in confinement.

"Get up Bashar, you are coming with us, now," one of the men said aggressively.

"Of course, anything you want," replied Bashar with his eyes down.

Bashar stood and put his hands behind his head with his eyes still facing down. He quickly got behind the man they pointed to and follow him out of the room and to the stairs. Behind him was three others, every one of them ready to beat Bashar if he made any stupid moves.

"Where are you taking him," shouted Jared from the next room over. Of course, they paid no attention to the American sticking his nose in other people's business.

Up ahead was a room with the door closed. The man in the front opened the door and turned towards Bashar, grabbing him by his shirt collar. Without hesitation, he pulled and then pushed Bashar quickly in the room and slammed the door. It was bright, Bashar had to squint his eyes while they adjusted. He was used to a dark room and had seen little light in the last seven years. There were radios and communication gear all over the room.

"Hello Bashar," came a voice.

Bashar still couldn't tell who it was and could only see the shape of a man. He stumbled forward, stepping into a chair. Bashar caught himself, while replying back to the voice.

"Hello," Bashar said timidly. "Why am I here?"

"Sit down Bashar, quit acting like your in a position to ask questions here. If it wasn't for me, you would already be dead. Adir wanted to skin you alive and put you out for everyone to see. How could you possibly begin to fathom that you are in any shape, in any position to give demands? Now do me a favor and sit down!"

Without hesitation, Bashar quickly sat down and put his head down, awaiting instructions.

"My name is Asim, I am Adir's top advisor. He wanted me to have a conversation with you, do you happen to know what about," asked Asim?

"The American," Bashar knew right away..

"That is right, I must say the rumors are true. You are quite bright, even after living in a small room for so long. The American is something we are extremely interested in. Even more interested in what his intentions are with our organization. Our anticipation is that eventually he will grow to trust you and share freely with you since he believes you are against us."

Asim pauses, staring at Bashar directly.

"However, that isn't true, is it Bashar? You would never turn against your people. You would never do more harm than you have already done to this family. You blame the local police for what happened, we know who really killed Adir's son. If it wasn't for the Americans, Amad would still be alive. Your imprisonment is only because of the blood money that was owed, that you did not have. That is the only reason you are still with us. I do have a proposition for you though."

Bashar head picked up, staring at Asim. He was suddenly interested in where this conversation was headed.

"If, Bashar, you are able to find out the American's true intentions, Adir has agreed to let you go and return to your home. There will be no repercussions and we will never bother you again. The debt will have been paid in full, no questions asked. What do you say to that Bashar? Are you willing to help your people, to ensure the safety and the future of our organization."

Bashar sat there thinking, wondering how truthful this entire conversation was. How could he take any chances though, with him knowing what saying no would surely result in? He couldn't live too much longer in his room, all alone, with nothing to offer the Army of Islam. He knew his answer immediately.

"Of course I will help the cause. Tell me what you want me to do," replied Bashar.

Asim smiled and explained the plan to Bashar.

♦

Hours later, Asim was once again sitting with Adir, talking about the future of the organization. Asim was excited and wanted to show Adir that he was taking care of the current situation at hand. He wanted there to be no doubt that the organization needed him and that he belonged in Adir's inner circle.

"He is completely on board, without hesitation. Any mention of him going home and getting out of here alive would surely get Bashar interested. How could it not? It has been seven years and he is still down there wasting away. I explained our intentions and briefed him on the plan ahead.

Everything is in order Adir, you have nothing to worry about."

"Thank you Asim, this pleases me. I appreciate your friendship and your honest advice," replied Adir.

Asim smiled, knowing he had come through and made his presence known. He stood up and started to limp out, briefly nodding at Adir with a silent thank you.

"One more thing Asim," Adir quickly spoke out.

"Yes Sheikh."

Adir stared at Asim with an evil look in his eyes, something that reminded him of the hatred that used to always be in Adir's eyes after his son was killed.

"If you screw this up, put this organization in danger, or put more of my family in danger, there will be no corner of this world you will be able to hide from me. I will make your entire family's name disappear from this earth, with no reminder that you or any of your generation have ever existed. Blood money will not be an option. Do I make myself perfectly clear Asim," asked Adir?

"Of course Adir" Asim quietly replied.

CHAPTER EIGHT

The Speech

August 16th 2019

Jared was being escorted back upstairs once again. He had been lying on his cot thinking about home when they came to get him. This time, only two escorts, maybe they were starting to trust him more. At this moment though, all he could do was continue to think about home. It was a dangerous path, one that he had to control from now on. Thinking about home made him sad, angry, irrational, and prone to making bad decisions.

Jared had been thinking about Linda and Albert, Katie's parents, before the escorts had arrived. They had always treated Jared with respect and love, never thinking twice about accepting him into their family. Linda was a typical southern woman, always wanting to make sure that others were fed with good home cooked meals. This meant a non-stop supply of care packages with great amounts of edible deliciousness. This kept Jared a popular person within the company, always having a sufficient supply of no-bake cookies and snacks from home.

Albert always treated Jared as a man, from day one. Without question, Jared and Albert hit it off from the first day that Katie brought him to her home. Jared being in the military may have helped that case, being from a small town in Tennessee there were only a few active duty military men. Jared enjoyed his company and looked forward to their trips to Tennessee to spend time with both Albert and Linda.

Jared was thinking about them and his family while lying on the cot. Both Cayden and Kaylee loved spending time with their grandparents. They had a swimming pool, a pretty decent RV, a golf cart to ride around in, endless fun for young children. Cayden could stay there forever, something that the autism likely enabled. He lived in the moment, didn't really care where he was at as long as he could live his life. The older he got, the more he missed his parents, but nothing like Kaylee. After a few days, she becomes homesick and longed to come back home. Without a doubt though, those two kids got lucky with those grandparents.

Cayden and Kaylee had been spending a lot of time with Albert and Linda, staying with them while Jared was deployed to Ramadi. Jared was thinking about them when they came to get him. His heart racing, his body aching for his children, he quickly wiped them from his mind and focused on the task at hand. Adir wanted to speak with him and sent less escorts to beckon him. Was it trust, or some sort of power play testing Jared?

"Hello Jared," Adir asked as they rounded the corner.

"Hello Adir, how are you," Jared asked?

"Fine, thank you," Adir replied. He motioned for Jared to sit down as he walked to his desk. Adir had wanted to bring Jared to his office, to show some sort of civilization. He was tired of the notion that The Army of Islam lived and fought in caves and backstreet alley's.

Instead, he wanted to present they were a well thought out institution. They had leadership, rank structure, rules and regulations to keep the army in line. Without it, they would basically be savages running around killing everything they could. This was not the case and he needed to show that to Jared.

Jared sat down, looking around the room slowly. He was in an office, obviously Adir's. There were pictures on the wall, a large map of Ramadi on the far side of the room, with markings all over it Along the back wall was a bookshelf, lined with books. In the middle of the office, where Jared sat down, was a table that could sit at least six people. In the middle of the table was documents and another map that was laminated and could be written on. What appeared to be what Jared would call an operation order sat on the table as well, shocking Jared that this organization took the time to elaborate on their mission and make preparations.

This had all caught Jared by surprise. Never would he had thought that the leadership of this organization had taken the time to collaborate and plan. This office looked almost identical to his own back in the states. Maps, orders, meeting areas, and books along the wall. Adir was intelligent, causing Jared to be a little more on edge.

"Jared, my friend, I have brought you here to have another needed conversation. Well, actually to ask you a question. An important question that I need you to answer, as we can no longer prolong what is happening here."

"Why do you want to join our organization?"

Jared knew this was coming and decided now was better than ever to have this conversation.

"Well Adir, that is a tough question. However, I understand your need to hear the answer and I am going to do the best I can to deliver. It's a long story, but I hope once I finish, you will understand my desire and why I have ultimately decided to burden you with my presence."

Adir nodded at Jared, as if telling him to go ahead and begin.

"Frankly, I am tired Adir, truly and utterly tired. I'm not just talking about being physically worn out, but a mixture of everything. Mentally, emotionally, and physically drained of my current nation. I'm angry, frustrated and ready for a change in my life. I find myself not wanting to live anymore, not wanting to push forward with whatever task is given to me, whatever unimportant mission is delivered to me."

"You see, I feel as though I have already proven myself in so many facets, that trying to show that even further would just place more burden on my shoulders. As an enlisted fighter, I have no place of authority. I always have to answer to someone, no matter what their experience is, or what they have or have not proven in their career. I have fought through five battles. In my fifteen year career, I have spent over six of those years in combat. I have fought in Iraq, Afghanistan, Africa, throughout countless battles. Countless firefights. Countless deaths. Fighting their wars, for their interest, with nothing in return. They can't even get the medals right. They just throw a piece of paper at you and have some officer shake your hand."

"Not many of them can fathom the loss some of us have endured. I have had men killed right in front of me, while having conversations. Do you know what that is like Adir? To be talking to a friend of yours, the one you have spent the last three years spending every single moment together with. Being out on a patrol for ten hours, and when you are finally heading back to camp to get some rest from the long day, your leadership wants to stop and talk to one more person. A person they think will make them look good with the right information. Then, while the leadership is talking to that one individual, while you and your buddy are walking around on security, your buddy gets shot in the head while telling you about his kids back home. All for some information!"

Jared shakes his head, obviously upset.

"I have literally had others call me illiterate, dumb, just a stupid grunt, or endless insults to fulfill their egotistic heads. They don't know that I have an education, that I understand tactics and warfare better than they will ever learn in school, or have been through countless programs to enhance my capabilities. Not to mention while they were still in high school or college, I have spent my time getting shot on three separate occasions, been hit by nineteen different IEDs, lost more friends in battle than I can count on my hands four times over. While they were dreaming of war, I was living it."

Jared lowered his head, shaken and angry at the conversation he was currently having.

"You see Adir, I came here not to join your organization. I came here because I need you to accept me. I need you to put life back into my empty soul. All I can hear is an echo, without purpose, my soul and spirit will never be fulfilled again. Not only that, I need you to help me make them pay. I am tired of this fake democratic rule over everyone. I want to make them suffer. When it is all said and done, I want to be the one standing over them smiling so they know that this dumb, illiterate, enlisted grunt was the one that brought them all down."

"What I want to see, what I need to see, is when they look up at me and realize I was the one that made them burn, instead of hatred and disgust in their eyes, I want to see fear. I want to see them shaking in pure, unforgiving fear. Can you help me get to that point in my life Adir?"

Jared stood up in his seat and leaned forward, getting as close to Adir as he possibly could.

"If you agree to help me accomplish that, what I have for you in return is irreplaceable. I will give you all their secrets. I will hand you all of their locations, all of their capabilities, all of their weapons, everything you can think of. You want it, I will give it. I will train your army, fight beside them, lead them in battle, and make them greater than they could ever imagine. I will create the most elite team in your organizations history. You see Adir, in my head, you can't possibly tell me no. How could you tell me no to this ultimate weapon I am giving you. I am offering you the one thing no other terrorist organisation has."

"I will be your greatest ally, ready to stand by your side as the greatest General the Army of Islam has ever seen. You will not be disappointed. I am ready to fight to the death for your beliefs and to achieve the greatest revenge we could dream of. You have no idea what I am capable of, how dangerous I am. You have no clue the things I know, the hate I carry. I can make this organization the greatest

terrorist organization on the planet. All you have to
do is say yes!"

Jared immediately turned his back on Adir,
and began walking as fast as possible, without looking
back. He was either about to get shot in the back,
yelled at, or nothing at all. He was taking a chance,
but Jared didn't, he had nothing to lose at this point.
Jared kept on walking. Down the stairs, past Bashar,
past the guards and went straight to his room and
shut the door behind him. He was still alive, so must
have gotten his point across. All he had to do now
was wait and see what the response would be.

♦

Adir sat there and watched Jared get up and
leave. He didn't say anything or direct his soldiers in
anyway. He knew this was theatrics and Jared was
trying to prove his point. The speech was good, but
he still had his doubts. He needed confirmation with

Bashar before he accepted Jared's plea. However, if Jared was speaking the truth, then the results could be game changing. This could catapult the Army of Islam into greatness, an unimaginable dynasty.

"Someone fetch me Asim, now," Adir yelled through his door.

Adir stood up slowly and walked to the window, grabbing the tea kettle from the ledge. He was grimacing in pain from his leg. As he poured himself some tea, he heard a soft knock on his door.

"Come in," Adir spoke.

Asim slowly walked in and closed the door behind him. "You called for me."

"Yes, I have just finished speaking to Jared and need to know if he is telling the truth. We need to ensure Bashar understands how quickly we need this information and how important his cooperation is to us."

Asim nodded and sat down at the table. He listened as Adir explained to him what his and Jared's conversation consisted of. Although understanding how important this was to Adir, he couldn't help but question Jared's motives. It all seemed too good to be true and Asim was never one to trust anyone.

He would ensure that Adir and the organization was safe though, even if it meant destroying everything he loved. He would never let someone ruin what he already had, especially an American feeling sorry for himself.

<u>CHAPTER NINE</u>

The Order

<u>August 17th 2019</u>

Staff Sergeant Hunter was sitting in the conference room, in one of the chairs that lined the back wall. The only enlisted Marine that sat at the table was the company First Sergeant, the rest were the officers along with the Commander. He had about three hours left before he went back on post, assuming his duties as the Watch Chief for the COC.

He guessed this had something to do with the attack on Three Bravo the other day and was ready to answer any questions that may arise. In the room with him was the patrol leader from the convoy, his Platoon Commander, Platoon Sergeant and some intel guys he hadn't formally met yet.

"Attention on deck," shouted the First Sergeant as he walked in with the officers and the Company Commander. An unnecessary action, they were in the middle of a combat zone fighting for their lives.

As the Commander came in, he told everyone to sit down, he was ready to get started. Straight to the point, he wanted to talk about the attack on Three Bravo. All eyes immediately flickered to Hunter And he started the initial brief.

"At approximately 1120 on 14 August, Mobile Assault Platoon Three Bravo's first vehicle struck an IED at grid JN47384-87437. Upon detonation, the vehicle was immediately disabled from the blast and they accumulated zero casualties. After securing the area and allowing EOD to examine the blast area, it was determined that the IED was a remote activated pressure plate designed to disable any vehicle driving over the initiation plate."

"Upon speaking to all parties involved, while also speaking with intelligence officials, it was determined that the remote device was possibly a cell phone and could have set the device from any location. There is no telling exactly where it was initiated, or if it was even turned on that day. This particular device could be set to active or non active, though we have no way of telling how long the device was actually armed. We can't even tell if the person who set it was even watching when the explosion went off."

"They were watching," the Commander injected. "There is no way they were not watching! There is something going on here and we need to be careful. Thank you Staff Sergeant," the Captain said as he stood up. He was walking towards the door when he stopped and turned around.

"We all know what is going on here and we need to stay vigilant. Leave the younger Marines out of this and ensure they remain unscathed from all of this. Division is in the lead for a reason and this all has something to do with Tremble. They have all of the control, we just have to adjust and prepare. I want everyone to cover their six at all times and act as though everything is going as planned in front of the Marines. If you hear anything out of the ordinary, bring it to me. Let me deal with the Division clowns, keep your hands clean."

As he walked out the door, he looked back and said "Hunter, grab Hayes and come sit with me!"

♦

Sitting in the Commanders small office outside the COC, Staff Sergeant Hunter didn't know what to expect. He had grabbed Sergeant Hayes and quickly they came to see the Captain. Neither had any idea what was going on, but they were going to find out soon enough. Something had the Commander upset, and Hunter was afraid they were about to catch the brunt of it.

"Gents,, how are we doing," the Captain asked as he walked into the office?

"Fine Sir," they both chirped back in response.

"Alright, let's make this simple. First, Hayes, nothing against you at all son. You have done an amazing job, we just need to add a little back up to your current situation. With Tremble gone doing God knows what, and having Division up my ass about everything happening in the AO, I felt this was a needed addition."

"Staff Sergeant Hunter will now be traveling with you as an advisor. You will still be in charge, making all the calls regarding the patrol. The Staff Sergeant will just be there in case Division has any questions regarding your patrol, ready to back you up and reinforce your decisions. This is not a judgement on your character, this is a tool to help you succeed against higher leadership."

Without hesitation, Sergeant Hayes quickly responded.

"Great Sir, I look forward to having Staff Sergeant along. Any assistance in this entire ordeal would be greatly appreciated."

"Simple enough, I am glad you concur. Shows how mature and mission oriented you are Sergeant. We are lucky to have you in our company! Staff Sergeant, do you have anything to add?"

"No Sir," Hunter replied. "I am excited to get back out on the road and letting Hayes run the show. Gets me out of the COC."

"Very well, if that's it, I'll let you guys get back to it," the Captain replied standing up. "Thanks for coming to see me gents."

As Hunter stood up with Hayes and turned around to leave, he couldn't help but wonder what he was just signed up for. There was no use questioning it, the Captain gets what he wants no matter what the cost is. He had no concern for getting back out in the fight, he was mostly worried he may have just been turned into a scapegoat for the company. If something went wrong out there, the highest ranking man would surely get the blame. Better him than Hayes though, Hunter would just be happy to get home alive. He just couldn't stop wondering if the Captain had other plans.

♦

"General Rogers, I did what you asked Sir."

"Thank you, Captain," the General replied.

"Is there anything else you would like me to do Sir," the Captain asked the General?

He had received a phone call last night from the General's aide, asking him to standby to speak with the Division Commander once he came out of his meeting. He didn't have a lot of time, so he needed the Captain to be ready as soon as he came out of the conference room. Of course, the Captain didn't really have a choice in the matter, the aide was just trying to make it easier on him.

After an hour and twenty minutes of waiting on the satellite phone, the aide said that the General was coming out now. The conversation was quick and straight to the point. As soon as the General got on the phone, he gave three tasks. One, talk with the Marines and find out who was the closest friend Gunnery Sergeant Tremble had in the company. Two, immediately put that Marine in Three Bravo for all patrols and any instance outside of the wire. Lastly, to keep a close eye on that Marine and report any unusual activity to the General directly. He was not to talk to Battalion about this, not to talk to his First Sergeant, nobody. Not even the General's aide. The aide was informed to immediately grab the General whenever the Captain was to call with information and not ask any questions.

"No Captain, your doing a great thing. I will ensure at the end of all of this, you receive your accolades. Don't let me down," the General responded.

"Thank you, Sir. I surely will not," the Captain responded.

Once the acknowledgment was given to the General from the Captain, the phone turned off. This was serious, and needed to be handled carefully. The Captain didn't like leaving the Company First Sergeant, or his own boss in Battalion, out of the loop. However, how could he ignore a direct order from the two star General himself. Not to mention, this was a great ticket to the top. As long as this entire evolution goes down as the General plans, the Captain had his ticket punched and ready for the future.

No, he wasn't going to ignore the General's orders, and will ensure he kept this tight lipped. He needed to watch his own back, and as long as nobody got hurt he would sleep just fine at night knowing he was doing the right thing.

<u>CHAPTER TEN</u>

The Deal

<u>*August 17th 2019*</u>

Major General Rogers was an experienced infantry officer that had commanded troops through countless battles. There were many wars on the forefront, some that were known and some that were not. Once he had become a Lieutenant Colonel, he was fortunate to take over a Battalion that was fighting in Fallujah and Ramadi within Iraq. Later on, once he was in charge of a Regiment, he commanded troops fighting in Afghanistan, Africa and others. He had earned his stars through combat unlike some of the others.

Now as the Division Commanding General, he had a plethora of items on his task list. Among those tasks, he had a Battalion currently in Ramadi fighting against The Army of Islam. Although the fighting hasn't been as intense as the earlier years of the war, there was still a fight at hand that needed to be won. The Army of Islam was a huge aspect in the current government relations, causing turmoil and fear throughout the country. Without having any control over their leadership, the future elections and any establishment of a civilized government function would surely fail.

General Rogers entered his conference room two minutes past the start time. This gave the rest of the staff enough time to be settled and ready to start once he arrived. This was the normal weekly brief from his major shops including admin, intel, operations, logistics, communication and funding. This normally took an hour to get through, and the General would not let it go past that. He rarely had enough time for the rest of his agenda and sitting here listening to his directorates trying to show how important their sections were did not sound like a good time to him.

"Who's first," the General asked as soon as he walked through the door?

"Good Morning Sir," the admin director stated as she stood. "This week we currently have no pressing issues. Your calendar appears to be normal in nature, without any major visits coming up this week. As asked, we have done a complete division accountability, and have all personnel accounted for...except for Gunnery Sergeant Tremble of course."

"Thank you Colonel," the General quickly responded. "Intel, your next."

"Good morning Sir, the Intelligence Community acquired additional and highly significant information regarding Abu Bakr al-Adir and Nawaf al-Asim from two years ago. Critical parts of the information concerning both individuals lay dormant within the Intelligence Community for as long as eighteen months, at the very time when plans for the attack in Paris were proceeding. The CIA missed repeated opportunities to act based on information in its possession that these two known terrorists were traveling to Paris. They also failed to notify French officials, alerting them to add both names to their current watchlists."

"Additionally Sir, it is known that after meeting with key operatives in Europe, al-Adir returned to Iraq three days before the attack took place in France. Thereafter, the Intelligence Community obtained information indicating that an unnamed individual, that we now know was al-Asim, was at a known location in Paris and had contacted a suspected terrorist facility in the Middle East."

"The Intelligence Community collected some of this information, but did not report any of it at that time. It was not reported because it was deemed not immediate terrorist-related, and nothing flagged the system deeming the conversation as a threat. It was not until after the Paris attack that the Intelligence Community determined that this information was directly related and should have been given to French officials."

As the Intelligence Director sat back down in his chair, the General just stared at him. Anyone in the room could distinctly tell by the look on the Generals face, he was nowhere near happy.

"I am obviously not going to shoot the messenger here, but you have got to be kidding me. We have a large scale attack happen in Paris, by an organization that we are aggressively following, where two of our own Americans are at and this is what we get from our intel. For goodness sake, these were our own people here. One of our Marines was at that restaurant when it went down. An American died because of that attack and we basically have nothing. A bunch of fancy words in the last two minutes that in simple terms means, 'we knew they were there, we could have stopped this, but we chose not to.' You have got to be kidding me."

"Yes Sir, that is right," the Intel director

responded softly.

"Let's move on, ops, what do you got," the General quickly responded by changing the subject.

"Good Morning Sir, we have normal operations going as planned. We have set up additional route clearance missions going during the night hours to assist in location, detection and removing of planted IED's. With the recent small ambush on Three Bravo in Ramadi this week, we want to ensure an effort is made showing the enemy that we are not getting complacent. We are also working on getting a day next week scheduled with a team and a flight to get you to their location Sir."

"Thanks Jim, no need for that though. I no longer will be traveling to their location through our guys. I already have a plan in place and I will continue to collect updates as we have been. Great call on the Dagger missions and setting up additional route clearance. Let me know how it goes and if we get an uptick in detected IEDs found."

"Yes Sir, too easy," the operations director responded.

As the General continued to listen to the rest of his morning meeting, he couldn't help but wonder if he was making the right move here. He had reached his current position through hard work, and fighting wars. He did that with his teams and trusted advisors. He normally didn't try to do his own thing and make decisions on his own. This time was different though, he needed to stay strong and stick with his initial gut feeling. He was successful in the past listening to his staff, trusting his advisors. However, his current position was also achieved off of the hard work and fighting spirit his Marines had put in.

What none of the Marines in the room, or anyone for that matter, had known was the deal he had made with the Company Commander from Weapons Company. He wanted to ensure that others were not involved, he had experience with having too many people involved that leads to altered messages and created confusion. He wanted information to flow directly from the Captain to him. This let the General make his own decision based on the facts he received from the Company Commander.

Looking back on the General's past, especially when he was a young Lieutenant Colonel fighting in Fallujah and Ramadi, he had never imagined himself in this situation. Not only was the Army of Islam starting to increase their capabilities and determined to enhance their global reach, but he also had a Gunnery Sergeant go missing in the middle of the night. There was enough speculation created from the media, the last thing they needed was an American epidemic of warriors switching sides for their own benefit.

So far, the media hadn't looked back far enough to put them together, but when the General was the Lieutenant Colonel commanding the Battalion in Ramadi the first time years ago, Gunnery

Sergeant Tremble was the machine gunner as a Lance Corporal in the General's truck turret attached to his Personal Security Detachment! If the media found that out, they may be able to start putting the puzzle pieces together. If that happened, then the entire operation would fail, this he couldn't let happen.

He gave Gunny Tremble his word. There was a debt to be paid and the General was going to make sure that it was paid in full, and then some!

CHAPTER ELEVEN

Flashback #2

August 8th 2018

Jared's eyes shot open, he stared straight up in the air. He could see the ceiling fan spinning above him. The low rumble of the box fan sitting on the dresser was continuous, a normal sound by now. The alarm on his cell phone was still buzzing, as he moved to turn it off everything in his body hurt. His neck, back, and shoulders felt as though he had spent the entire night holding a forty pound ammo can over his head. This was the life he had chosen, no need to complain, but it still sucked.

As he looked at the cellphone, he noticed it said six, early for a Saturday. He must have been in auto mode last night and set the alarm as if it was a weekday. Sometimes he did things that he didn't understand. He had been so tired lately, the last thing he wanted to do was get up early on his day off. He felt like he was tired all the time, never fully getting rested throughout the night.

He spent two to three hours a day conducting physical training, doing high intensity workouts and hitting all of the major muscle groups. Something he tried to do daily, focused on straining his body pretty hard every day. He never wanted to be unprepared for the least expected, but his body was starting to feel the effects of constant strenuous fitness programs. He continued to tell himself, what if something happens today?

He was up now, so he might as well get the coffee started. He sat up slowly, trying to stretch the stiffness out of his sore muscles. Everything popped throughout his body. He couldn't even imagine how he would feel at fifty, if this is how thirty three felt. As he stood up, the family labradoodle was standing at the end of the bed. Baylee might as well have been their third child, as Katie treated her as such. She thought he was going to work, so she had plans on stealing Jared's pillow as soon as he left the bedroom. She was pretty much Cayden's only friend, so Jared let her get away with a lot.

As Jared walked out into the kitchen, the first thing he thought about was the children. He quickly lifted the full pot of water already staged on the Bunn. He poured it into the top, starting the coffee brewing process. Jared was not one to wait for something, so Katie bought the Bunn to make the brewing process faster. As the pot took its three minutes to brew, Jared walked to the children's bedrooms to check on each one of them. You never knew what could happen throughout the night, one of the things that haunted him. He checked on Kaylee first, to make sure she was still in her bed. Jared always had the fear that the kids would stop breathing in their sleep, so the first thing he did every morning was put his hand on their chest to feel the rise from taking a breath. She was fine.

Jared then walked into Cayden's room, like every other morning and spotted the disaster of a bed called Cayden. He was a rough sleeper, known to have the entire bed in shambles from twisting, turning and wrapping blankets around his body. He also had a thing for covering his head with his blanket, which always made Jared a nervous wreck. Cayden was fine though, as Jared was careful not to wake him up. As he headed back to the coffee, Jared picked up the laptop to check the news from last night.

There was always something going on and Jared felt as though there was always bad news being reported. He wished he could one day read some good news, but apparently that wasn't breaking news. Another shooting, another young soul taken too soon, the morning was already starting off with a dreary overcast. As Jared sipped on his coffee, he looked up and seen the calendar. That was right, he had already forgotten. Today was the day he needed to take Katie to get her passport for their trip. As much as he wished she would forget, he knew that wouldn't happen. Jared just had to be careful and ensured everything was planned carefully. This would be easy, especially with no kids.

Jared finished his coffee and headed back to the bedroom. It was now seven and he had no idea where the last hour had gone. He may need to get that checked. He crawled back into bed and slowly put his head down on Katie's chest. He could lay there all day, listening to her breath and rubbing her slowly. He was happy with his life and knew he wouldn't have it any other way. Things had changed and he knew it. It took some getting used to while deployed, but when he is in the states, Jared noticed he could not sleep without Katie in the bed with him. It could be nerves, anxiety, or separation issues, but if Jared was home and Katie was elsewhere for the night, he could not sleep at all.

She stirred awake and looked at Jared. "What are you doing awake Jared," she asked?

"I set my alarm for some reason last night. I couldn't tell you why, but I must have been on autopilot mode. So I woke up at six."

"That sucks," Katie stated.

"At least we can get ready and get to the post office early. We need to get the passports on order, you never know how long they will take. As soon as we can get a date of arrival for the passports, then we can set a departure for vacation," Jared said.

He likes to get things done and out of the way. The sooner they get the passport done, the better he will feel on the planning aspect for Paris. Katie stirred more awake and stretched herself.

"Sounds good to me. I am ready for anything. You tell me what we need to do and I will help us get there."

She was always a trooper and was no stranger to hard work and dedication. She pushed Jared's head off of her chest and sat up in bed. As she stretched more, Jared went back to his side and grabbed his phone. As he started to look up the hours of operation for the post office, Kate stood up and walked towards the bathroom. As she started to pull off her clothes, she said she was going to take a shower before they got going. Jared grunted approval and waited for her to disappear in the bathroom.

Once she was gone, his search went from the post office, to the current dangers in Paris. He would never be able to ease his mind, but he wanted to be fully prepared. When Katie thought of Paris she pictured tourism, attraction and romantic dates. When Jared thought of Paris, he pictured explosions and terrorists. His head was full of turmoil.

He had always felt he needed to be the one that protects his family. He was the Marine with the training, he had been in multiple situations where empathy disappeared, and pure hatred replaced it. He had always known that if someone threatened his family, especially his kids, he would end up doing terrible things. Just thinking about child kidnappings or traffickers made him go insane. He could just envision the things he would do that would eventually send him to prison. That could be some old feelings from the wars creeping back in, but without a doubt Jared knew that if he needed to enter a world of darkness to protect his family, he would go there in an instant.

He had recently watched a video on Facebook that showed a woman walking past a family of four and out of nowhere she stabbed a young boy in the face twice. Jared could not even fathom what would cause a woman to do such a thing, but he couldn't control the thoughts that ran through his head. For instance, why didn't the dad sacrifice everything to stop her, or after the incident take her down and detain her? Why didn't he grab the knife and live by the old ritual of an eye for an eye? Also, Jared would think about why she would do such a thing. There had to have been something bad in her life that caused that to happen, but then Jared started to wander. Thinking about protestors and watching domestic terrorists chasing down little girls calling her names crept into his mind. Before he knew it, Jared's heart was racing and he became angry at the world.

He thought about walking into the bathroom and trying to talk Katie out of going to Paris, possibly Disney World again. The kids loved Legoland, it would be a perfect vacation. Jared knew better though and quickly realized that possibly he was making things worse in his head. That Paris wasn't a deathtrap and plenty of Americans visited there every day.

Jared stood up and began to get dressed, preparing himself for long lines and endless requests at the post office. He would make an effort not to complain and see how quickly he could get a passport for Katie. As he walked into the bathroom, he heard the water to the shower turn off. He lathered up his face and began to shave as Katie dried off. He wanted to make an effort.

"You know Katie, I have been thinking about this trip," Jared said.

"Oh yea, let me guess. You think it's a bad idea," Katie quickly responded.

"No hun, thank you. Actually, I am pretty excited about the whole thing. Collecting stamps in our passports, seeing the world. This is why we love the military, getting to travel. I think this is going to be a blast."

Katie appeared to be shocked, just staring at Jared with a puzzled look on her face.

"Well, good," she responded, acting as though she didn't quite know what to say.

"Alright hun, I'm going to go grab the kids out of bed and start getting them ready. I am going to tell Cayden we are going to Buffalo Wild Wings afterword, so hopefully he won't mind the lines," Jared said as he walked out of the bathroom.

"Okay," she yelled back to him.

I think that went pretty good Jared thought to himself as he walked to the bedrooms. He would never tell her that he thought she was putting them in danger, he wanted her to have a great time and look forward to her trip. He knew what could happen, but what were the chances of that anyway?

CHAPTER TWELVE

The Class

August 17th 2019

As Jared sat in his room, he began to wonder how this would all go down. He was having second thoughts about getting up and walking out on Adir. It was possible that the difference in their cultures could have caused some turmoil, although Jared was only trying to prove a point. He should have thought about that move more, instead of making choices while working through emotion. Too late to second guess it now, there was no going back in time.

"Jared how are you doing over there," Bashar asked from the next room over?

"I'm okay Bashar, how are things going on your end?"

"Quite fine, thank you," Bashar quickly responded.

"The other day, when they pulled you out of your room, where did they take you," Jared probed Bashar?

"They allowed me to talk to my family, those I haven't seen in a long time. There is actually an opportunity for me to leave here, to finally go back home," Bashar said excitedly.

"Fantastic news," Jared responded quickly.

"Yes, it is. I am very excited about the whole thing. How have things been going on your front? Have you received any insight of joining their organization," Bashar asked?

"Not yet, but I have a plan. I have told Adir why I want to join, the reason why I have gone through this trouble. Of course, I haven't told him quite everything, but why would I at this point? They want me to trust them, but won't give me their trust," Jared stated.

"Interesting, what else do you have left to tell them? I thought you were going to lay everything out in the open and see what happens," Bashar quickly responded.

"There is one more aspect to my reasoning behind all of this, but it has to do with my family. Something I want to keep just for me, but if I have to use it and tell them I will. Please keep that between me and you Bashar, I would like that information to not be shared openly, if you know what I mean."

"Of course my friend," says Bashar.

Suddenly, without notice, Jared's door opened with a guard standing in the open doorway.

"Asim would like to see you."

"Fine, do I need to bring anything," Jared asked the guard?

"No, just yourself," the guard replied.

As Jared stood up, he looked around his room as he instinctively wanted to grab a pen and a notebook, but nothing was there. No change of clothes, no books, not even a jacket. Maybe this situation would change, one could only pray.

Jared quickly followed the guard through the stairway and halls, wondering what he was being called upon for now. He wished he had known how long it would take for him to find out his fate, he was sick and tired of sleeping in the small closet they called his sleeping quarters. If they accepted his plea, his offer, his living arrangements may actually get better.

After they went to the second floor, the guard stopped, pointing towards a closed door. Jared, not sure what to do, gave the guard a questioning look, just asking for him to give some sort of direction. The guard stared back and shrugged, while turning around and leaving. Thinking that was odd, Jared opened the door and walked into the room. What appeared in front of him was a large, open room. Lined with tables and chairs, it looked similar to an open classroom layout he was used to in the states. There was nothing on the walls, with one light in the very center of the ceiling. He quickly recalled that this was the room they had met before, when he set off the IED on the American convoy.

Standing in the back was Asim, smiling at Jared. He motioned for Jared to come towards him, to come closer.

"Welcome to your new job," Asim spoke out.

"I don't think I am understanding you," Jared replied.

"Well, you spoke your mind to Adir and he believes in what you are saying. I may not agree with him in this aspect, but that's not for us to discuss now. Adir has decided that you will begin instructing classes to our new recruits, teaching them the skills needed to defeat the American Infidels," Asim told Jared.

"What do I get in return for doing this," Jared asked Asim?

"Nothing."

"What do you mean, nothing," Jared quickly responded.

"You are alive, we are feeding you, you have a place to lay your head and sleep at night. What else would you want from us?"

"Well, I would prefer to move to a better room, one that I can begin to collect things I would like to have. Paper, pens, books, just different things," Jared responded.

"How about, for now, we settle with life," Asim coldly spoke back.

Asim continued, "Go through this classroom, tell us what you need to make it this happen. Make us a list, we will see what we can do."

"Very well, by the sounds of it, I don't really have a choice," said Jared.

"No, you do not," Asim spoke as he began to walk out of the room.

Jared was getting where he needed to be, he had to have more patience to continue down this path he was traveling. Jared walked to the middle of the classroom and sat down, thinking about what he needed to make this happen. He needed to get out of the mindset of an American classroom. Instead, he needed to imagine what would work best in his current situation. He also needed to embrace his foreign weapon experience, as this would be crucial to his success. The better this instruction turned out, the better his conditions may get.

THREE DAYS LATER

August 20th 2019

Jared had received his list of essential items and spent the last twenty-four hours setting up his classroom. He was ready to get to work and solidify his spot within the organization. He was a little uneasy about how the recruits would react to an American providing instruction, but he was ready to get started.

Jared had placed maps, paper, pencils, a projector, a dry erase board, plus other items throughout the classroom. He was determined to create this new era within the Army of Islam, becoming well known for shaping the future. Jared was going to be known throughout the organization, one way or another.

At exactly 10:00, they began to filter into the classroom, ready for Jared to begin his period of instruction. In the back, sat both Asim and Adir. Jared needed to ensure he performed well in this first test. Adir had his wooden crutch today, he must be having a hard time getting around with his leg.

"Good morning everyone, my name is Jared. As you can tell, I am an American. Back when I first joined the military, over a decade ago, there wasn't a single thing about me that would scream warrior. I was young, dumb, and always thinking I was better than everyone. Then I deployed to Fallujah and learned pretty fast that I wasn't the warrior, instead I was facing them."

"Experience made me into a warrior, firing that first round that took some other fighters life. Surviving in a place that wasn't meant for survival. That one shot, the first one ever, the one you know hit its mark, is the turning point that takes you from the young dumb kid, to a warrior of blood."

"Now I know what everyone is thinking, what's on everyone's mind at this very moment. I am an American, one that spent years of my life fighting against you! Let that sit in for a moment, let the hate inside of you build to the surface."

"So what does that make me? It makes me damn dangerous! I know what the other side is like, what they do, their desires, their tactical immediate actions, everything. I am a weapon that you and your organization have never had the chance of having. I have the ability to make each and every one of you the most ruthless and ferocious killers out there."

"Now that I have your attention, let's talk about the overview. We are going to discuss

Command and Control today. I want to start off by showing you how to control the battlefield and accomplish small missions. This is done with technical and organizational attributes, employing multiple resources like technology, human, and informational tools. We are going to set organizational goals and lastly talk about solving problems and accomplishing tasks."

Jared began to walk around in front of the large classroom as he began to feel more comfortable, much like the old days as his time as a School of Infantry instructor.

"We have no learning objectives today and the media will be us discussing the objectives using this projector and dry erase board, along with constant conversational discussion between all of us. You have unique skills that I have no idea about, that mixed with my expertise will make you a dangerous group of individuals."

"There will be no evaluations, some practice runs outside and no safety concerns today as we will not be using live fire weapons as this time. Are there any questions on what we are going to cover, how we will cover it, or what you will be expected to learn?"

No hands went up.

"Great, let's get started," Jared stated right away.

Both Asim and Adir stood up in the back and quietly walked out the door. Jared smiled inside, knowing he hit the mark with his opening remarks.

Jared began to teach his classes holding nothing back, knowing he was molding the future terrorists of the world.

<u>CHAPTER THIRTEEN</u>

The Traitor

<u>*August 20th 2019*</u>

After Adir and Asim left the classroom, they headed upstairs to their planning and operations room. They had to discuss future operations for the organization, which now would include the American Jared.

"We need to put him and those recruits in a hard situation, one that he will be forced to prove himself," Asim spoke out loud.

"I agree, Asim, a planned ambush on a convoy that isn't just a roadside bomb. I want Jared and the recruits to get face to face with the other Americans and prove their worth," replied Adir.

"However, before we do that, I need you to talk to Bashar and see what he has to say about Jared," Adir said while looking at Asim.

"Very well."

"Let's continue with the planning process," replied Adir.

Pointing to the map, Adir found the perfect location ten kilometers away that Jared and the men could set up the perfect ambush. This would not draw any attention to 3-Story, while allowing the group to inflict as much damage as possible.

"This is the location, I want the plan to come from Jared and the men. One month from now, is when they will perform the ambush. Prepare Jared, tell him we want all of the details and to be properly briefed on what he will be doing. Now go speak with Bashar and see what he has to say," Adir said to Asim.

"Sounds good, I will report back when I am finished."

♦

"Hello Bashar," spoke Asim, who was standing in his doorway.

Bashar sat up on his bed slowly, feeling drowsy from lack of exercise and little light.

"Good day, Asim," he replied.

"So Bashar, what information do you have for us?"

Bashar had been thinking about this for some time now. He had been speaking with Jared off and on for ten days now, with the American being nothing but nice to him. Bashar knew his time here was limited, no matter what the response here was.

Not to mention, there was nothing to tell Asim, Jared wasn't openly speaking about overthrowing the organization. What was Bashar to tell Asim, that there was something about Jared's family that he wasn't telling them. Bashar didn't even know what that meant directly.

"Well Asim, I have been speaking to the American now for some time, the last week or so. Quite frankly, there is nothing to report, nothing to tell you. He seems to be genuine about his request.

He has spoken to me about why he wants to join the organization, due to the way the American leaders have treated him. Nothing has come from him that is negative in nature against the Army of Islam."

"So Bashar, you think his intentions are honest?"

"I really do Asim. I even hear him in there studying material, practicing his classes for the next day. It sounds as though he cares about what he is doing, maybe even giving him a little bit of joy. I would trust him, I think he is trying to help your organization here," Bashar told Asim.

"Great, thank you for doing your part Bashar," Asim responded back.

"So does this mean I am free to leave?"

Asim stared at Bashar, smiling coldly. Turning around and walking away, he spoke as the guard shut the door.

"Bashar, this means that Adir will not kill you and your family. You leaving though, that will never happen. You must not be as intelligent as I gave you credit for."

Bashar put his head down, knowing that hope was nothing but bad news with him. He had actually thought he had a chance to go home to see his family. Once again though, he was being punished by Adir for something that was out of his control.

♦

"Bashar says he believes Jared is sincere. I believe him as well, from what he reported to me. I think we should tell him about the ambush and see what plan he gives us," Asim reported to Adir.

"Very well, what did you tell Bashar?"

"I told him to sit tight, he wasn't going anywhere. He should be grateful he is still alive."

Adir turned away, wondering what he should do. He had to give Jared this shot, to see how it would affect the organization. What if Jared pulled through? Adir would be known as the greatest leader in the organizations history. The one that turned an American into an allied weapon. He would give Jared a chance, to see how effective the American can be.

<u>CHAPTER FOURTEEN</u>
Flashback #3

<u>*September 23rd 2018*</u>

Jared was finishing up in the shower, preparing for their date. They were staying in Okko Hotels Paris Porte De Versailles, a nice but affordable four star hotel within Paris. Katie had already showered and was finishing up her makeup. He had never seen her so happy before, smiling from ear to ear over everything she saw. From arriving at the airport, to getting transportation to the hotel, she just kept looking around and smiling. Jared felt accomplished and was proud that his mission on getting Katie to Paris was turning into a success.

They were a little tired from the trip, but instead of going to sleep, Katie had wanted to quickly get out and have dinner at L' Auberge Aveyronnaise. She was so excited about getting dressed up and going out. She had seen things like this in the movies, but had never imagined she would be doing such a thing within her lifetime. Her friends had married doctors and engineers from back home and were always posting on social media with their fancy cocktails and expensive and lavish lifestyles. One day, Jared would give her all of that, after the fighting was done.

The kids were staying with their mimi and wepaw, Albert and Linda, and were having a blast. Of course Jared and Katie missed them like crazy, but there was nothing to worry about. The kids loved being there and with it being September, the weather was nice and endless outdoor activities was in session. The grandparents love spoiling both of them and the children couldn't ask for anyone better. Jared knew they were in good hands and never questioned their safety. Both grandparents would gladly give their lives for either child and that's all that mattered to Jared.

"Are you about ready Katie," Jared yelled out to his wife?

"Yes, I am coming out now."

As Katie walked out of the bathroom, Jared could barely remain standing. She was dressed in a stunning black sheath column off-the-shoulder floor length satin dress. Jaw dropping wasn't the word for it, Jared was stunned.

"Do you like it," Katie asked shyly?

"Of course, you look absolutely amazing. God only knows how I got so lucky to have someone like you as my wife."

"Now stop it," Katie laughed. "But thank you."

"Are you ready to head to the restaurant," Jared asked?

"Sure am," she replied.

As they rode the elevator down to the ground floor, Jared couldn't take his eyes off of her. He was so shocked, he had never seen her like this before. He couldn't shake the feeling, that feeling of attraction, pure love. He felt the same as he did 12 years ago, if not more in love with her.

As the elevator reached the bottom floor, they stepped out and began to walk out of the hotel. Jared was able to immediately flag down a les taxis parisiens and head to their destination. Jared held open the door, helping her get the bottom of her dress all the way inside the cab. Jared stepped in on the other side and told the driver their location.

On the drive towards the restaurant, Jared and Katie talked about their future. They had big dreams, all revolving around Jared retiring from the military and starting a new career. He envisioned having at least four incomes, his military retirement with disability, his new job, her job, and his writing career. He figured with this, they could be comfortable and live a life they have always dreamed about.

Nothing extravagant, they wanted to have things like a boat, a set of jet skis, things of that nature. Hard work and patience, was the key to Jared's success in his mind. Five more years and they would be done with all of the fighting. He had his degrees and certificates, he just needed the five years to come to an end.

Once the cab arrived at L'Auberge Aveyronnaise, Jared jumped out and ran around to the other side. He opened the door, helping Katie out of the vehicle. As they walked in, Jared spoke with the greeter at the front and they were immediately taken to their table that Jared had reserved on their flight. Katie was impressed.

Jared helped Katie out with the ordering aspect, but she was only entertaining him, it was pretty easy to order and she could have managed all on her own. She always did things like that to make Jared feel as though he was helpful.

"Are you happy Jared," Katie asked him as they settled in?

"Of course, why?"

"I just wanted to make sure, I am well aware that you don't like to do things like this, that it makes you nervous," Katie responded.

"Oh I'm fine," Jared stated. "I just want to keep you safe. I start to wonder about what could happen, how things could go wrong. I understand the chances though. I know that the likelihood of something terrible happening is slim to none. Like I said, I just worry too much."

"I know hun, I appreciate you thinking about that kind of stuff, working hard to keep us safe. More than you know, I appreciate it," Katie replied.

"We should do something like this every year Katie, someplace new and exciting. Save up some money and travel the world. We should have one goal, to fill up our passports and see where we can go."

"That's a great idea, I would really enjoy that. Maybe next year we can go to Mexico, see what is going on down there," stated Katie.

"That sounds pretty cool, looks like our food is coming," Jared pointed towards the bar, as their waiter had a serving dish filled with plates of food.

Behind where the waiter was walking, something caught Jared's eye. Nothing out of the ordinary, sort of like a stir of people. It seemed as though more people than normal all stood up at once at the far side of the restaurant. It could be nothing, maybe there is a sporting event happening.

Jared settled back down in his chair and welcomed the waiter with their food. Jared was hungry and could not wait to dive into some great French cuisine. Suddenly, back over where the initial group of people that had stood up quickly, there was some more movement. People were now rapidly spread out and moving away from a certain location, some consisted in loud shouts and even a scream or two.

Jared was now fully aware something was wrong, something was happening at this very moment. Jared scooted his chair back hard, hitting the table behind them. He did not care, he had one concern at this very second.

"Jared, what are you doing," Katie demanded!

"Katie, get up. Now!"

"Why Jared, what are you doing?" she asked again?

"Katie!" Jared responded, looking right into her eyes.

She knew something was not right with that remark, quickly standing up and doing as he said. Jared grabbed her arms and began to pull her to the rear of the restaurant, towards a back exit. Somebody stood up and tried to grab Jared and see if everything was alright. Without a sound, Jared quickly shoved the man back into his table, hard! There was no time for this, Jared had to get Katie to safety, then he would return and try to assist others.

"Katie, we are almost out," Jared said as he turned around to look at Katie.

That's when the bright, blinding, white light filled the entire building in an instant.

CHAPTER FIFTEEN

The Request

August 22th 2019

It was day twelve of Jared being with the Army of Islam. He was a fast learner, able to pick up on cues and react the way he thought he should. Some of the recruits would actually come up to Jared and ask him questions at the end of the day, picking his brain on random inquiries. Much like the Marine Corps, they were eager to learn, eager to fight for their beliefs.

It amazed Jared at first, but after a day or two, it became normal, like he had never left and was still back teaching his junior Marines. Adir would watch throughout the day, seeing their future evolve in front of his eyes. Jared had even taken the building plans of the new Patrol Bases built by his unit and hung them on the wall. He often referred to them when giving his classes.

Jared was finishing up with his classes today, mostly spent talking about the defense. He discussed how the Americans would set up, build, and defend their location throughout the city. Again, referring to the Patrol Base plans helped, often showing the students first hand what he was talking about. Not only did it enable them to understand, but made them believe in him more, actually make them feel he was trying to be one of them.

"So that is why you set up your obstacles, in order to try and channel attacking forces into straight lines. You create an opportunity for enfilade fire, having a better chance of defending yourself against larger forces. We will get more into that tomorrow by discussing beaten zones and how to employ open bolt weapons into your defense. More importantly, we will discuss how to take a defense like this and overcome it. If there are no more questions for today, I will see you early in the morning."

As the students stood up and began to leave, Adir appeared from the back of the room.

"Jared, once you have finished cleaning up, come join me for dinner. I want to talk to you about something," Adir spoke to Jared.

"Understood it shouldn't take me long."

After Adir left the classroom, Jared walked around the room and ensured everything was in place. Jared knew that Adir was adamant about objects being in order. He didn't want to walk in and discover a mess or be perceived as "unprofessional." So Jared made sure every evening that the room was clean and organized before leaving.

Jared left the classroom, while locking the door behind him. Instead of taking the usual left turn to head to his room downstairs, he took a right and headed towards the end of the hall where the dining area was. Jared never actually went there, he was always brought some sort of tray throughout the day. He hadn't figured out if they didn't want him to wander alone through the building or if it was part of the hospitality in their culture.

As he arrived at the dining area, he seen Adir sitting at the very end of the hall by himself. This was interesting to Jared, as he assumed that Asim would also be here.

"Come, join me Jared," Adir said waving him over as he noticed Jared walking into the room.

Knowing they would probably eat, Jared walked over to the sink and washed his hands. This wasn't his first time with Iraqi etiquette and Jared knew what he was supposed to do. He knew not to pass or touch food with his left hand. He knew to cut fruit into slices as he ate, and he knew to accept all food given to him. This was the easy stuff.

"How has your day been Adir," Jared asked as he sat down?

"It has gone fine, thank you," replied Adir.

Adir offered Jared some tea, which Jared gladly accepted, holding his hand over his heart thanking Adir.

"So Jared, you have been doing quite well here, giving great instruction to our new recruits. Your contribution to our cause has not gone unnoticed."

"Thank you Adir, I truly appreciate that," Jared responded.

"Now that you have been here for a few weeks, do you have any questions for me? Anything that you cannot figure out and would like to ask me?"

Jared hesitated, obviously thinking about his response.

"There is one questions Adir," Jared responded after taking a quick sip of his tea.

"I cannot figure out one thing around here, even after talking with the recruits. It's as if nobody wants to tell me. Who is the actual leader of the Army? I haven't seen anybody that I would perceive that is in charge of the entire organization. I assume you are possibly in charge of this clan, but who is the overall leader?"

"Well Jared, we are only the group within our organization that lives in Ramadi, but we are spread far and wide throughout the region. I am not in charge of anything, I just oversee the training piece here in Ramadi. I meet with our organizational leader once every few months, maybe more if he requests it. He chooses not to live here for the fear of an overhead missile attack on 3-Story."

Adir paused, drank some of his tea, and set it back on the table. With a small rag in his hand, he wiped his mouth.

"To be completely honest with you though, you are nowhere ready for that level yet. The leader knows about you, but has not spoken to me about what he wants to do with you yet. He understands your current commitment, how you are helping train the fighters that will attack the Americans here. We need to see how that goes first."

Jared didn't understand, which was obvious by the look on his face that Adir quickly caught onto.

"Well Jared, we thought you would have figured it out by now. The recruits you are training, they are here for a reason. You will be leading this group of fighters in an attack on the Americans. You are training them specifically for that purpose. You will either live and be a huge part in our history, or you will die and be forgotten about. Your choice, your will."

Jared did not expect this to be the case and was caught off guard. Quickly recovering, he looked at Adir.

"Understood Sheik, I will not disappoint you. I am ready to lay down my life for the beliefs of The Army of Islam, 'Insha Allah'.

CHAPTER SIXTEEN

The Ambush

September 22nd 2019

JARED

"Today, is the day, where you make your family proud. Today, is the day that you make Allah proud. Those guys over there, they are going to try and take your life. They are going to do whatever they can to make you leave this world on their terms, not your own. If you are not ready to make the sacrifices necessary to win today, then walk away now."

"We are not here looking for glory. We are not here for a win. We are not here for some sort of joy. We are here, to show the world, that the Army of Islam can and will claim all religious, political, and military authority worldwide. We are done telling them, we are done threatening, it is time for the real deal. Now let's go show them!"

Jared was actually proud of this group. He had just over a dozen individuals that he had turned into an elite fighting team. They were staged ten kilometers north of 3-Story waiting for the American convoy already traveling towards them.

The last week had been spent preparing for this moment. They were ready and had everything set up. They had an explosive device set, three ambush teams already in place and Jared was staged in a three story building so he could control the entire conduct of the ambush. Jared was about to prove his loyalty to the Army of Islam.

SSGT HUNTER

Staff Sergeant Hunter was sitting in the rear seat behind the driver in the second vehicle. Three Bravo had been directed to go on a presence patrol, to look at a specific building. The call had come from

Division, odd for such a routine patrol. Hunter didn't pay too much attention though, there was quite a bit of weird going around the last six weeks.

"How far are we out Hayes," Hunter spoke into his head set?

"Looks to be about 5 minutes," came the reply.

Easy enough. They were to go to the building labeled AG341 on the division map, drive around it while taking pictures of the North and South side, and return back to base. Easy mission, they should be back in time for dinner.

Hunter wasn't used to simple though, and fully expected some sort of hiccup. This was Hayes' show though, no reason to step in and create fear. He has his own way, time to let the next generation step up.

JARED

The call came in, the convoy was three minutes out. Jared took a small red flag and pushed it into a small hole within his window sill where he was standing. This told the three teams that the attack was about to begin. All three would now be at the ready, waiting to hear the explosion and start the attack.

The idea was for the IED they had planted to hit the first truck, forcing the rest of the convoy to stop behind it. Once that occurred, the first team would initiate contact to the rear vehicle, forcing the entire convoy into a kill zone trapping all four vehicles. Once the kill zone was established by the first team, the second team would initiate contact onto the West flank of the patrol.

This would cause the dismounts to get out of their vehicles, through the East side. By doing this, it would expose the backside of the Marines as they returned fire to the West.

That is when the third team will engage the Marines from the East, effectively catching them returning fire to the other team. The Americans were trained for something like this, knew not to dismount and get stuck in a kill zone. However, poor leadership would at times instill panic and loss of control. This is what this plan was designed for. This is also what Jared briefed Adir and told him to expect.

SSGT HUNTER

The building was up ahead, on the left. Hayes had already started taking pictures of the building.

"Don't get sucked into the mission Hayes. Make sure you are paying attention to the details around you and let someone else take pictures," Hunter offered to Hayes.

"Makes sense, my bad Staff Sergeant."

Hunter was already nervous. The company leadership already made bad decisions with the mobile sections, as it was a last minute effort given to them during the RIP_5, or Relief in Place.

The Commander didn't know they were getting four vehicles, he just assumed that Weapons Company would be handling all of the mobile patrols. That wasn't the case though, as the company showed up to their camp, there sat four vics for them to use.

Hayes had been a machine gunner for a deployment with Weapons Company and knew how to operate mobile sections. The downfall, the company didn't train enough drivers, being forced to use drivers from past deployments. This ended up being a majority of their machine gunners. This meant that the machine gunners were all driving, while the mortarmen were all firing the machine guns through the remote system. You couldn't ask for a worse scenario.

They began to pull closer to the building. Hayes was speaking on the radio with Division, so Hunter grabbed the camera and began snapping pictures of the building. Up ahead was some rubble in the road, Hunter didn't like to take chances.

"Hey man, tell the first truck to watch out for that dirt pile up ahead," Hunter spoke to the driver.

"Got it Staff Sergeant," the driver replied, slowing down.

Suddenly, there was a bright light and smoke in the air up ahead, followed by a deafening explosion.

There was shouting from the Marine operating the turret.

"Truck one hit, truck one was hit!"

Hayes began to shout on the radio, telling the COC that they had just struck and IED!

JARED

"Damn it, I missed," Jared yelled to the first team on the radio. "Initiate contact to the rear."

As soon as Jared stopped talking, he heard the rapid onslaught of their AK-47's, 7.62 rounds flying through the air hitting the rear of truck four. He knew they wouldn't penetrate, but it would serve its purpose.

The IED had missed its mark, going off early before truck one had reached the mark. This was common for command detonation though.

Everything was going as planned, Jared was happy. He had one more trick up his sleeve though.

SSGT HUNTER

"Hayes, it's an ambush. They are hitting us from the rear, what are we doing?"

As the smoke cleared, it appeared as though truck one hadn't actually gotten hit. The IED had gone off early.

"Return fire damn it," Hunter yelled to the gunner.

"It won't fire," came the reply.

"Move!"

Hunter jerked the gunner out of the seat. Immediately, Hunter scrambled up into the center of the truck and slid into the gunners seat. In front of him was the M2 .50 Caliber, ready to rock and roll. Jerking the system to life, Hunter began to return fire. Outside, they could hear the easily recognizable thump of the heavy machine gun. As soon as the other trucks heard it, they began to return fire as well.

"We have got to get moving, get us out of the kill zone Hayes."

Suddenly, a red flash appeared on the remote screen. Hunter moved the joystick around slightly, trying to see what it was. Then another. Hunter seen where the second flash came from, appearing to be a figure standing up in a third story window. It wasn't an RPG though more like a red star parachute flare, nothing that would cause any damage to their convoy.

JARED

Jared had just popped his second red star flare towards the convoy, knowing it would get the attention of Hunter. The machine gun on the turret slowly turned and pointed at Jared. Jared stood there, and then put his arms up in a wide shrug, like he was telling Hunter he was an idiot. Jared wave his right arm as if telling Hunter to drive off. Push the convoy through the kill zone and get out of here.

Jared grabbed a third red star parachute, popping it right at Hunters truck. The second fire team had begun firing on the West side of the convoy, trying to trap them in the kill zone. Jared slowly turned around and began to walk down the stairs so he could leave the building. He needed to get to his team before someone sees him actually helping the American convoy. Not like it mattered, Adir and the organization were about to find out Jared's true intentions.

SSGT HUNTER

It was Tremble! Hunter could tell right away who it was, completely shocked. It was like Jared was trying to tell him something, trying to get Hunter to do something. There was intense fire coming from two sides now, two different enemy positions. In the background, Hunter could hear Hayes telling his men to dismount.

"No," screamed Hunter! "Tell them to stay in the trucks. Push out of the kill zone and get the hell out of here."

"We have a mission Staff Sergeant."

"Not anymore. Get this convoy moving before I throw you out of this truck and leave you here to complete this mission by yourself."

Finally, the convoy pushed out, leaving the madness behind them. The gunners were returning fire and calling in fire missions to the COC. They had almost been entrapped into a deliberate ambush. It would have worked too, if it wasn't for Jared Tremble.

CHAPTER SEVENTEEN

The Truth

September 23rd 2019

"They performed well, didn't they Jared?"

"Yes they did Adir, I am very proud of them," replied Jared.

"What would you do differently?"

Jared thought about this, careful to answer the right way.

"We need an expert, a subject matter expert on explosives. Command detonation and pressure plates are predictable and are easy to miss with."

"You are right, of course. I will talk to Asim right away, I will ensure he gets an explosive expert in your training and joins your team."

"Thank you Adir."

Adir leaned back in his chair, happy with yesterday's work. He had called Jared to his room to discuss yesterday's assault.

"You know what Jared, I have something to tell you. Something I have been holding back from you for weeks now. I no longer want to be dishonest with you brother," Adir slowly said.

"Ok, Adir. Whatever it is, I will understand."

"The truth is, I lied to you about the leadership of this organization. I didn't want you to know the truth, know what was really going on here. The actual truth is, I am the leader of the Army of Islam. I am the one making all of the decisions. I had a feeling about you, which led me to overturning all of the others concerns about you," spoke Adir.

"Ramadi is the main focal point of our operations, I have a far reach but it originates here. I actually took over the organization a year ago, on this day. I designed and carried out an important part of our history earning me the position of the organizations leader."

"Really Adir, what was it," spoke Jared? There was a small tremble in his voice.

"Last year I planned a large scale operation. It involved an attack on a location that killed thirty seven people, earning me the right to lead. Through countless days and nights I planned and orchestrated the devastating coordinated assault."

As Adir spoke, he appeared proud. His chest was out, speaking as if he was running for re-election. He stood up, beginning to walk around the room, boasting about his attributes.

Jared asked a question, "Where did this offensive take place?"

Adir turned around slowly, smiling with pure happiness and joy inside. "In a Paris restaurant called L' Auberge Aveyronnaise, on September 23, 2018!"

♦

FLASHBACK #4

September 23, 2018

L'Auberge Aveyronnaise

The explosion was tremendous, with the heat almost unbearable simultaneously. Jared couldn't see anything as the room filled up with smoke. He could faintly hear the screams of the guests, all reacting to what just happened.

Jared was on his back, with debris that appeared to be the remnants of a wooden table on top of him. He slowly pushed it off, trying to stand up. His head hurt, his nose bleeding. He tried to clear his head, but that was near impossible.

"Katie, where are you," he barely whispered?

Jared still could barely see a foot in front of him, but he had to find Katie. She could be trapped, buried under enormous piles of debris. Finally, Jared was able to stand up.

Jared stumbled forward, looking on the ground around him after each step he took.

"Katie, can you hear me?"

Somebody ran into him, Jared quickly grabbed their shoulders and pull them back from his chest. He looked in the person's face, not Katie!

"Go that way, through the back exit," Jared told the woman while pointing towards the door.

"Katie! Hun! Where are you? Can you hear my voice?"

No response, only the screams of the unaware. Those reacting in the moment. Suddenly, there was more than just the screams! Gunshots began to rapidly fill the outside of the exits. Jared turned around looking at the back door he just told the woman to run too. There she laid, bleeding from multiple areas on her chest.

Jared hit the ground, using the smoke and darkness for concealment. He began to low crawl towards the back door, looking for the gunman. More shots! More screams!

A man with a gun came through the back door. He looked around for a few seconds, then began firing rapidly through the entire building. He wasn't aiming at all, his intent was to get as many rounds to bounce around the inside of the building as possible. There was no regard for his own safety, as he wasn't paying any attention to those around him. Good, Jared thought to himself.

Jared continued to low crawl towards the door, taking a wide approach as to not cross the gunman's path. There in front of Jared laid a table leg sheared at the end. Weapon of opportunity!

Without thinking, with zero hesitation, Jared grabbed the table leg and stood up. He was to the immediate right to the gunman, who didn't stand a chance. Jared stood and took two big steps forward, jabbing the table leg into the right side of the man's throat. As soon as it went into his throat, Jared dropped the leg and reach for the AK-47, ensuring the man didn't turn and shoot towards Jared as he died. The man didn't get the chance, as he quickly bled out, dying without movement.

Jared grabbed the weapon, pulling back on the charging assembly to check the weapons condition. It was ready to fire, so Jared stepped through the back door with the weapon at the ready. As he cleared the doorway, there stood two men firing AK-47's towards the front of the building, both of their backs to Jared.

Jared pulled the trigger and the weapon jumped to life. Three rounds in the back for each man, they died quickly. As Jared stepped over them, he fired a few more rounds each to ensure they were gone, he didn't have time to check. Jared continued to the front of the building. As he rounded the corner and entered the main street area, there was a man to his left. The man was getting into a black sedan with a weapon slung over his shoulder. Jared took aim and fired his own weapon.

The 7.62 rounds ricochet and impacted the sedan. One round hit the man's right leg through the back of his knee. He fell into the sedan as it sped off, someone closing the door after pulling him in. Jared grasped the trigger and held it down as the vehicle drove off, emptying the magazine into the rear.

Jared threw the weapon down and sprinted through the front door, still looking for Katie.

"Katie! Katie!"

People were running past him, out of the front door. Jared pushed his way through, trying to find his wife. There were people laying all around him, bleeding everywhere. He began to look at each face trying to find the love of his life.

That's when he saw her. Laying on top of a broken table, not moving. As Jared slowly stepped forward, he began to shake. Katie had been shot multiple times in the chest. She was bleeding profusely, not standing a chance. Jared bent down and check her pulse, already knowing the answer. She was gone, likely bleeding out almost immediately from the impacts. Jared began to sob, knowing he had just lost his wife.

All he could think about was their children, how they would react. He couldn't believe this had happened, that they were here when this attack occurred. Jared took a nearby table cloth, covering Katie up. He couldn't see her like this anymore, he was devastated that he allowed this to happen to her.

As Jared stood up and walked out the front door, the anger that built up in him was indescribable. He knew he was going to kill every person involved with this. He would dedicate his entire life. Nothing would stop him. There was one thing Jared knew for certain, whoever was responsible for killing his wife, would be erased from this world!

CHAPTER EIGHTEEN

The Revenge

"Yes Adir, I know," Jared responded as he stood up slowly. "I know about that attack, quite well actually."

Adir spun around, looking at Jared with a puzzled look on his face.

"You see Adir, I was there that day, I was in Paris. I was in that very restaurant, eating dinner with my wife. Her name was Katie Tremble. She had a beautiful family, with two beautiful children. Because of you, Cayden and Kaylee will never be able to see their mother again. They will never hold her, cry on her shoulder, tell her their problems with boyfriends and girlfriends while growing up."

Jared took another step towards Adir, pulling a small Makorov pistol out of his back pocket. A 9x18 caliber pistol, it had an eight round magazine inserted.

"Katie Tremble, was one of the thirty seven people killed in your ambush. She was shot and murdered by your ringleader, Asim. I know that because I am the one that shot him through the knee. I was the one that watched him get into the balck sedan after I put a bullet through his leg."

"Katie was forced to spill some of the blood that made you the leader of this organization. Katie paid her life, so you could rise in the ranks. My family suffered, so yours could prosper. Isn't that right Adir?"

Adir stepped back, obviously scared about what was happening.

"Jared, I didn't know! You must understand brother…"

Jared pulled the trigger eight times, rounds jumping from the pistol into Adir's chest. All eight impacted, taking the breath away from Adir, not allowing him to finish talking.

"I am not...your...brother. You are nothing Adir. You are nothing, but death!"

Jared stood over Adir, watching the light leave his eyes. As he died, relief washed over Jared, knowing this was the beginning. This wasn't the end though, he needed to hurry. He ran towards the door.

Jared peered out through the hallway. He knew he had to run down the hall to his right to get to the communications room. To get there though, he had to go right past Asim's room and there was no way Asim didn't hear those shots. He had to get to the communications room though. Asim was also due to meet Jared at this time, as Jared was certain that Asim was there that day. He needed to finish off Asim with what he started a year ago for pulling the trigger that killed Katie.

Jared was sure that Asim's limp was from him shooting the man getting into the van. Why wouldn't he be here as Adir's second in command, after doing the dirty work for Adir that day in Paris. Yeah, Asim will get his and Jared had just the plan.

Jared had no more ammunition for the Makorov, but there was a fixed blade knife in Adir's desk. It resembled a K-Bar and would assist Jared in defending himself. He walked over and opened the drawer, grabbing the knife. As he walked back to the door, he slid it into the back of his pants. He peered out the door into the hallway again, checking to see if anyone had come upstairs yet. There was nothing, as gunshots wasn't uncommon in the area.

Jared stepped out into the hallway and took three steps towards Asim's room. Jared looked around one last time and began to shout.

"Asim, quick, hurry. Someone shot Adir. He is bleeding badly. I am not sure how long he has!"

Jared began to force himself to breathe hard, bending over and putting his hands on his knees. A few moments later, Asim came out of his rooming, frantically staring at Jared.

"Jared, I thought they sounded close. Where is he?"

"He is in his room. I heard the shots and walked up the stairs. I seen him laying by his desk with his door opened. Hurry!"

Asim began to rush down the stairs, limping badly on his right leg. He appeared to be hesitant, but it could just be the leg. Asim went past Jared and walked into Adir's room.

Jared stood up in the hallway, slowed his breathing, and pulled the knife from his pants. He slowly walked to the edge of the door, preparing himself for another fight. He suddenly skirted the edge and rushed into the room so he could kill Asim.

As soon as he turned the corner, Asim was standing there facing the door, with his own pistol aimed right where Jared came in at. Jared dove to the left as the shots began to fire towards him. He got behind the second desk that was on the left, bracing for impact.

One round had caught Jared in the side, blood slowly soaking through his shirt. It wasn't a through and through, but merely a cut through his flesh.

Asim was no longer firing shots, so Jared peered around the corner to see where he was at. No one stood there. Jared jumped up, still holding the knife. Asim must have left the room, heading to get more ammunition.

Jared peered out into the hallway, there he was, liming down the hall. Jared took off at a dead sprint, intending on tackling Asim from behind. Right as Jared was about to hit him, Asim spun around with a machete he took from Adir's wall and tried to hit Jared. The blade had missed just over Jared's head, allowing Jared to finish the tackle and take Asim to the ground.

On the ground they began to struggle. Jared had lost his own knife when he made an impact with Asim. Jared tried to punch him in the face, but was blocked by Asim's arm. Asim jabbed his own large blade at Jared's chest, missing to the right.

Jared quickly stood up, making some distance between him and Asim's blade. There was a small table against the wall in the hall. Jared picked it up and smashed it on top of Asim.

"You were there that day, weren't you Asim," Jared asked?

"Of course I was. I was always there for Adir. I am going to be here for him now, by avenging his death and making you suffer in the process."

"I am afraid I cannot allow that Asim," spoke Jared. "I owe you your own piece of suffering. I owe you pain, for the death of my wife"

"How do you know I was the one who killed your wife. I was only there to oversee everything, not actually the one killing innocent lives."

"It doesn't matter Asim."

Asim stood up, slowly backing away from Jared. He grasped the large knife tighter, slowly putting his hands up.

"If it doesn't matter, then I might as well tell you the truth. I was the one that pulled the trigger and killed your wife. I wanted to be the one that killed the American whore. I shot her six times and enjoyed every second of it. Now I am going to finish the job and kill you as well. When I finish taking care of you, I might send a team to get your family as well for what you've done here today."

Without hesitation, Jared lunged forward holding a table leg in his hand. Asim swung the blade at him, Jared catching it with the leg. As Asim raised the large knife again, Jared kicked his right knee hard, dropping Asim to the ground. Without hesitation, Jared shoved the table leg into his left knee, through to the other side.

Asim screamed in pain, dropping the knife as he grabbed his left knee, trembling from the pain.

Jared had tears in his eyes, knowing what he had just done.

"Tell me Asim, was it worth it!"

Jared quickly grabbed the blade, sliding it quickly across Asim's throat.

As the light faded in Asim's eyes, he slowly nodded. Jared stood up wiping the tears away and began walking down the hall to the next room. He threw the blade behind him as he approached the door. He went into the communications room and turned on the single channel radio. He quickly programmed the right frequency into the radio and keyed the handset.

"This is Gunnery Sergeant Tremble. Zero...Nine...Two...Three. I repeat. Zero...Nine...Two...Three.

<u>CHAPTER NINETEEN</u>

The Cavalry

<u>*September 23rd 2019*</u>

"Alright boys, that's the signal. Three Bravo, mount up," yelled General Rogers!

◆

The General had arrived at Command OutPost Elmore at 0600 without notice. As he rolled in with a total of ten Mine-Resistant Ambush Protected vehicles, the camp immediately stirred awake. The General was in a hurry, demanding the entire company leadership to meet him in their conference room.

At 0615, the General asked the Company Commander if everyone was present. The response quickly returned as a "Yes Sir."

The General stood in front of the conference room, standing at a staggering six feet five inches. With a large frame and years of infantry warfighting muscles, the General was very intimidating. Also in the front were over a dozen Special Operations Marines, none of them saying a word and standing by waiting for the General to say his piece.

"Alright gentlemen, here's the deal. Since the night of August 11th, we have been tracking Gunnery Sergeant Trembles every move. This was a plan he brought to me himself, that I quickly agreed too. The Gunnery Sergeant and I go back to the early days of the war and it's a shame of what happened to him and his family."

The General began to pace back in forth in the front of the room, showing this would be a while as the General gave the background.

"On this day, exactly one year ago, Gunnery Sergeant Trembles wife, Katie, was brutally murdered in Paris. On that day, the Army of Islam named their current leader, Abu Bakr al-Adir. He orchestrated the attack on the Paris restaurant that killed thirty seven civilians. One of those civilians was Katie Tremble, while they were on their international vacation."

The room was deathly quiet, the jaws of the Marines dropped, staring shockingly ahead.

"Gunny Tremble came to me and told me the situation and requested to go on this mission. We have already been watching the Army of Islam since that attack and had them on our radar. After discussing the plan with the Gunny, I approved and assisted in the entire operation. No one knew but the two of us."

"We set up the ambush on Three Bravo yesterday, as this was Gunny Tremble's time to prove his allegiance to the Army, in order to get close to Adir today. Once Tremble achieved that task, he is to give a pre-designated signal over a single channel radio. He ensured that all members were safe in yesterday's ambush, which is why he was the one that set off the IED early. He also requested Staff Sergeant Hunter to go on that patrol, as he knew the Staff Sergeant would see him and understand his attempt to get you guys out of the kill zone."

"Later on this morning, on the frequency I will provide, Gunnery Sergeant Tremble will be calling in a four digit code to signal us that he is ready for us to roll into his location and initiate our own clear phase. This will be a kill and capture operation, we expect heavy resistance. Remember we have an inside man, if anything happens to Tremble inside that building, I will ensure everyone of you are placed behind bars until I see fit. Any questions?"

The Company Commander stood up, "Sir, who will be going with you on this op?"

"Three Bravo, personally requested by Gunny Tremble with Staff Sergeant Hunter. They will use my vehicles that I brought with me, as well as the Marines up here in the front with me. The Master Sergeant to the left here is in charge, but Three Bravo will accompany and fill the seats. Three Bravo will be doing the assault. So Saddle Up!"

♦

The General shouted for everyone to get in the vehicles, the signal was given. He had heard Jared's voice himself give the signal, he was ready to get his Marine back.

"Staff Sergeant Hunter, your in my vehicle," the General yelled!

"Yes Sir!"

The General climbed into his truck, the second one of the convoy. He was behind the driver, Staff Sergeant Hunter was behind the Vehicle Commander, the Master Sergeant from the conference room.

"All VICS roger up when your ready to push," spoke the Master Sergeant over the radio handset.

Without hesitation, the response came

through. Hunter could tell immediately these were squared away heavily trained Marines.

"Truck 1...UP!"

"Truck 3...UP!"

"Truck 4...UP!"

"Truck 5...UP!"

"Truck 6...UP!"

"Truck 7...UP!"

"Truck 8...UP!"

"Truck 9...UP!"

"All VICS, truck 2 is up, Oscar Mike," responded the Patrol Leader. Oscar Mike was often used to signify "On The Move."

The vehicle pounced forward, heading out the gate. The building they were heading to was about fifteen minutes away, at their current speed they would be there in seven minutes. Dangerous way to travel in Ramadi, but time was the current enemy.

As they sped along, the General was thinking about Jared and what he must be going through right now. He had lost his wife one year ago to the day and had spent the last six weeks living with the Army of Islam.

He had to do certain things to prove his loyalty, but Jared had no idea that he had not hurt any Marines in the last six weeks. Jared was likely sure he had killed some of his brothers, the General could not wait to tell him that wasn't the case at all.

Without notice, there was an eruption of smoke and dirt ahead of their vehicle, truck one had hit an IED in the road. There was no talking though, as the Marines were well trained. Truck two quickly sped around truck one, with the rest of the convoy following them. Truck ten stopped, set up security and checked on the casualties. They were now down to eight trucks, with about four minutes remaining.

The General grabbed his radio handset attached to the seat in front of him. He began to speak into the handset that had the frequency to all of the trucks in the convoy.

"Gentlemen, this is General Rogers. I want to personally thank each and every one of you for being a part of this operation today. None of you had to do this, but instead chose to on your own free will. For having a one day notice and nobody but myself knowing about this entire op, that is truly remarkable. It shows your love for your fellow brother and his family."

"Personally knowing Katie Tremble, I know she would be proud of each and every one of you for the sacrifice you are willing to make today in order to make these demons pay."

The General unkeyed the handset and took a deep breath, before going back to talking to his Marines.

"We are about to embark on an organization that truly hates who you are. They hate what you believe, what you love, what you are willing to do.

You know what I'm saying? Good! Go ahead and hate me too for not telling you about this operation, it just makes sending them to hell that much easier. Anyone who is okay with killing dozens of people trying to eat with their loved ones, I am perfectly fine putting them six feet under."

"Look to your left. Look to your right. These are your brothers. These are the people in this world that are willing to give their life for you. They are willing to take a bullet for you and send one down range to protect you. We are the most elite, we are the tip of the spear, we are the ones who are about to exterminate the Army of Islam from this earth!"

The General put his handset down and grabbed his weapon. The troops were pumped and ready for a fight. The General was confident in his men, he just didn't know how many he would lose today.

"Alright Hunter, let's do this. Let's get Jared back home," the General said looking to his right as they rounded the corner at a high speed to 3-Story.

Staff Sergeant Hunter looked over at the General just as the RPG hit the Commanding Generals window!

CHAPTER TWENTY

The Friend

Jared had sent his signal as planned, but he needed to get to the roof of 3-Story so he could act as the guardian angel overwatch. The last thing he needed was the men he had just trained for the last six weeks to set up an ambush and take out his quick reaction force he had just summoned. Jared still had the surprise on his side, as the only people who knew the truth about Jared was already dead. It wouldn't take long though for them to figure it out, Jared needed to be ready.

The armory was all the way downstairs on the base floor, past Bashar's and Jared's room. Also down there was the berthing area for half of the team Jared had been training. Three flights of stairs, in the armory, then back up to the roof. Easy!

Jared ran out of the communications room and took a left towards the stairs. As he ran down the stairs one of the men was coming up. The man nodded at Jared. Returning the nod, he muttered, "Forgot my notes in my room, I'll be in the classroom in three minutes."

Jared reached the bottom of the second set of stairs and began to walk past Bashar's room. He was looking through the bars on his door, as Bashar wasn't a free roaming individual within the compound.

"Hello Jared," Bashar spoke as Jared rushed past.

"Hello Bashar," Jared returned.

"What happened, are you alright?"

"Of course Bashar, why do you ask," Jared quickly responded?

"Well, you have blood all over the side of your shirt."

Crap! Jared forgot about the wound he received from Asim. What was he going to tell Bashar? He had an idea, it was crazy, but worth a shot.

"Simple Bashar. I just finished killing Adir and Asim upstairs and have called my people to come take down this building and this organization. I was sent here as a spy to infiltrate this organization and kill the leaders. They killed my wife a year ago today, this is my revenge."

Jared stood back, waiting for Bashar's response. Bashar looked shocked in his room, Jared was about to turn away and just leave him locked up so he wouldn't get in the way.

"Jared, let me out. I can help you finish this. Just promise me you will let me leave this place and go back home to my family after we are done. Please!"

Jared smiled, looked around the hallway. The keys to the door were hanging on a hook on the other side of Jared's room. Grabbing the keys, Jared unlocked Bashar's door, letting him out.

"Bashar, half of the men I trained are in that berthing room past my living quarters. We have to get to that armory first, gather some equipment and weapons and get back up to the roof. Nobody knows what is happening yet and I need to keep it that way."

Just when he finished speaking, a group of four Army members came through the berthing door, preparing to head upstairs. Bashar quickly backed into Jared with his hands behind his back. Jared caught on quickly.

"Come on Bashar, Asim wants to talk to you upstairs. Get your ass moving before I bust your teeth out!"

Jared jerked Bashar around as if he was going to hurt him, all while the four men walked past them and upstairs. As soon as they cleared the stairwell, Jared let go of Bashar. They pushed forward to the armory, quickly before more came out of the berthing area. As they walked past the entrance to the berthing, Jared had an idea.

"Bashar, throw me those keys!"

Jared caught the keys, then stepped towards the door and locked it closed. It wouldn't last long, but it would give them a few extra moments to get what they needed and head up.

Jared unlocked the armory door and slowly pushed it open. In front of him was an assortment of weapons. What Jared needed was a few rifles for close quarters and a precision fired weapon. What layed to the right of the armory was just what he needed, or would at least make do with what he had to choose from. The Dragonov rifle would be what he carried to the rooftop and protect his brothers, the Marines.

The Dragunov is a semi-automatic, gas-operated rifle with a short-stroke gas-piston system. Firing a 7.62 x 54R round, it would pack a punch. Next to it was a case, which he opened looking for a sight. He had taken a foreign weapons class long ago as a Sergeant. Trying to remember what optic went with what rifle was difficult, but not impossible. The case contained a PSO-1 optical sight, which Jared knew immediately is what he needed.

Jared grabbed three 10 round curved box magazines, a case of rounds, and a sling. As he was preparing the Dragonov, he shouted to Bashar.

"Brother, grab two of the AK's and all of the magazines you can. I had the recruits pre-fill all of the magazines, so grab as many as you can and throw them in a bag. Those AK-47's have slings on them, grab those."

Bashar did as he was instructed. Jared looked through the armory for one more thing. Yes, there they were. Asim had got his hands on a small lot of Russian F1 grenades. He began to put them in Bashar's bag, knowing he would need them when the time came.

"Alright Bashar let's get moving."

As they walked from the armory and past the berthing, they heard banging on the door.

"Let's move a little faster Bashar!"

♦

"General Rogers, are you alright," Hunter was yelling to his left. The RPG had hit hard, without notice. Everyone seemed to be fine, although the General wasn't responding. He was moving around over there though, so Hunter wasn't too worried. He had to get the Marines in this fight before it was too late.

Hunter left his vehicle and peered up at 3-Story. Members of the Army of Islam was on the roof, firing at the eight trucks. Hunter took aim, standing behind his vehicle and began to return fire. He emptied an entire magazine before ducking down behind the cover. He changed magazines and looked around.

"Let's go warriors, get your ass in this fight. We are not here as friends, they are *shooting at you!*"

Hunter stood back up and returned fire again, hitting one of the enemy fighters in the stomach. The Marines had left their vehicles and was returning fire now, gaining fire superiority over the enemy and taking control of this fight. Suddenly, Hunter saw the General running with the Special Operations guys and going in the building. Hunter left from behind the vehicle and jumped in the rear of their formation.

♦

Jared and Bashar reached the top the door that led to the roof.

"Alright Bashar, on three. They are out there fighting, so we have to surprise them and take them out before they know we are on the other side."

Jared slung the Dragonov and grabbed an AK-47 from Bashar. Inserting a magazine, Jared racked the charging handle to the rear. He threw three more magazines in his pockets and grabbed two of the F1's. Cracking the door, he quickly pulled the safeties and armed the grenades. Sliding the door open, he threw one to the left and one to the right before closing the door back shut.

"Alright Bashar, 1...2...3!"

As they rushed through the door, both grenades had gone off killing a handful of fighters on the roof. There was still five left as Jared and Bashar began firing their weapons at the enemy fighters.

♦

The team heading into the building had made the breach. As they rushed into the first floor, they began to spread out and check the rooms. As they passed the first two empty rooms, they came to a locked door. There was banging on the other side, so they couldn't take the chance of them breaking through the door and getting behind them. The team set a breach charge on the door and stood back.

As soon as the charge went off, the Special Ops guys cleared the room, killing three men inside who had weapons and were going to fire on them. The last two surrendered, so the team secured them and left two of their own behind to watch them and secure the first floor. As they left the room, they saw an armory on their right.

"Staff Sergeant Hunter, drop this in that room as we prepare to leave the building. Stay with these two, they will let you know when to drop it."

The team leader handed Hunter an M14 Thermite. Then the rest of the team headed up the stairs.

CHAPTER TWENTY ONE
The Fight
<u>September 23, 2019</u>

The sounds of gunfire filled the hallways. It was nearly impossible to determine which direction it was coming from. Staff Sergeant Hunter was still waiting by the armory with the two other men, waiting for the command to drop the Thermite inside.

Hunter had taken a knee, taking cover behind the heavy armory door. He had no idea of how this building was structured, so he could not anticipate where any enemy fighters would come from, if any. He had seen his own people go up the stairs on the far end of the building, that was the only entrance he remembered seeing, a door at the bottom of the stairs. Basically, when you entered the front door, you either go straight ahead to the stairs, or take a right and come right at Hunter.

Staff Sergeant Hunter leaned forward slightly,

peering to the left attempting to see the other two Marines in the berthing area. He could see one in the prone, off set from the door at an angle to maximize his point of view while achieving as much concealment as possible. Hunter couldn't see the second man, but had to assume he was doing ok.

Suddenly, a shout of gunfire and ricochets enveloped the hallway. It sounded as though there was impacts right next to Hunter's head. He fell backwards into the armory, sliding to his left behind the wall. He had no idea where the enemy shooter was located, or how many there were. At this point, all he could assume was they knew where he was and was continuing to fire on his position.

As Hunter sat there against the wall, he prepared himself for a fight. He slowly came off the wall and aimed his M4 carbine at the open door, preparing for an Army of Islam fighter to run through the door. Momentarily there seemed to be a lull in the shooting, likely a reload. This was his chance, he had to make this one attempt in eliminating the current threat. Hunter had no idea where this person was even at, but like he told his young Marines all the time, hesitation gets you killed. Time to go!

Staff Sergeant Hunter sprung to his feet, settled his M4's buttstock firmly in the pocket of his shoulder and breached the open doorway straight into the hallway. Looking over his optic slightly, he looked down at the end of the hall towards the stairs, nothing. He walked steadily down hallway by himself, looking in each room as he went. Still nothing, he was unable to locate the enemy shooter, there were no sounds of gunfire either.

Had to be the stairs, he needed to act quickly. Hunter picked up speed, still looking over his optical sight as he held the weapon up. The stairs was five steps away. Three more to go. Last one, hit the corner and prepare to engage. As soon as Staff Sergeant Hunter turned the corner to the stairs, he saw the fighter. Laying on the stairs on his back, there was one gunshot in the middle of his forehead. A steady stream of blood flowed down his face onto the stairwell, obviously he didn't survive.

Staff Sergeant Hunter slowly turned around, looking back towards the berthing where the two Special Operations Marines were at. One stood in the doorway, looking at Hunter with a smirk on his face. He gave Hunter a single wink, turned around and went back inside the room. Hunter smiled back, laughing out loud immediately. He could only imagine what he looked like going down that hallway, especially with the two other Marines in the berthing room watching him walk right past them as if they didn't exist.

Staff Sergeant Hunter gathered himself back together, stepping down the two steps he had climbed as he turned the corner. He let his M4 fall down in front of him as he turned to go back towards the armory room, he still had a task to do. Destroying the armory was an important factor to ensure other Army of Islam fighters didn't get to the stockpile. He began to walk slowly back to his position.

Suddenly out of nowhere, an explosion at the front door sent Hunter sprawling through the air!

◆

Jared and Bashar was still on the roof when the explosion went off. All of the Army of Islam fighters that were on the roof were gone, leaving the rooftop clear. Jared had just started walking towards the edge of the building to get eyes on the road when the explosion went off, shaking the building. It came from the area the front door was at.

Jared ran to the edge and peered down to the road. There was a group of at least twenty people down there, all with weapons. There also appeared to be three trucks with heavy machine guns mounted on the back, all aiming towards 3-Story. He needed to get down the stairs and defend the second floor. If all twenty fighters came in the building, Jared and Bashar wouldn't stand a chance on the roof.

"Bashar, come here," yelled Jared! "Stay down behind the ledge. I want you to fire your weapon down at those men on the street. Take their attention off of the building and focus on you. Stay behind the ledge so you have cover to protect yourself. I need time to get down the stairs and secure the stairway, making it easier to defeat them. I'm going to leave the Dragonov with you!"

"Got it brother. Be careful, Jared. Rid this world of these truly evil people, Insha Allah," Bashar responded.

Jared began to walk towards the doorway to the stairs with his Ak-47. Bashar stopped him.

"Jared, wait," he shouted.

Jared stopped and turned around. Bashar was standing there with his hand out, in order to shake Jared's hand.

"Thank you for letting me out, for giving me a

chance to go back to my family brother."

Jared shook Bashars hand.

"Of course shaqiq," Jared responded. "Your going to be fine, I'll see you soon."

Jared turned and went towards the doorway. He grabbed the handle and prepared himself for what he may find behind the door. His right hand was on the pistol grip, finger laying over the trigger guard ready to fight. With his left hand, Jared yanked the door open quickly, only to be met with five rifles pointing right at his face.

"Why hello Gunnery Sergeant Tremble," came a familiar voice.

"General Rogers, always a pleasure," Jared responded.

"You sure have caused a little bit of a mess here wouldn't you say?"

"Maybe a little Sir, nothing we can't quickly clean up," Jared respond smartly

The General smiled, "Well let's get to it. Let's end this, for Katie."

"Yes Sir!"

CHAPTER TWENTY TWO

The Clear

September 23rd 2019

Hunter moaned as he tried to stand up, the blast had sent him ten feet down the hallway. He could faintly hear gunfire as his ears began to regain the ability to hear sound. As he looked up towards the armory, he could see the two special ops guys firing over his head towards the doorway. One was waving at Hunter with one hand, trying to tell him to crawl towards them to cover.

Hunter began to crawl, even though everything in his body hurt. He didn't know if he was hit or not, no time to stop and check. Reaching forward, he forcefully pulled himself towards the other two. They were still firing rapidly. The one that had shot the fighter earlier and winked at Hunter reloaded his rifle, taking a few more shots towards the door. He stepped forward and came towards Hunter, grabbing his collar and pulling him back. Suddenly, the Marine pulling Hunter was hit twice in the chest, falling down to the ground.

Hunter could feel pain throughout his entire body, no longer able to pull himself forward. From behind Hunter, a grenade flew over his head and rolled around behind the other Special Ops Marine, exploding behind him after bouncing off the wall, send him through the air towards Hunter. Hunter knew he didn't have much time left.

He dropped his rifle and turned over onto his back, as he no longer needed it. He could see five enemy fighters firing in his direction. Suddenly they stopped and began to slowly walk towards him. Hunter knew they were going for the armory, likely to grab more ammunition and weapons.

Hunter reached down into his cargo pocket, grabbed the Thermite grenade and pulled in out in the open. One of the enemy fighters pulled up his weapon and fired at Hunter, hitting him twice. He quickly grabbed the safety clip, ripping it from the grenade and pulling out the safety pin, he let the lever fall off the incendiary. He quickly threw it backwards over his head, towards the armory as he bled out on the ground.

♦

Jared and the rest of his team started to clear down the stairs, heading towards the bottom floor and the front door. They quickly cleared the third floor and headed down the stairs to the second.

"There is a berthing area and a classroom on this floor. The fake patrol base plans you gave me are hanging up in the classroom. There is no telling how many people are left in the berthing area," Jared shouted to the front.

"We already cleared the berthing area on our way up," yelled General Rogers.

"Time to go gentlemen," the Master Sergeant yelled, pointing towards the dining area at the end of the hallway. Black smoke was slowly rolling towards them down the hallway.

The group headed towards the stairs and began to clear down towards the bottom floor. As soon as they reached the bottom half of the stairs, they began to meet resistance. Jared and the group began to return fire, gaining superiority quickly. Jared looked back to the rear of the group, giving them a nod. The last two men grabbed incendiary grenades and threw them down the hallway on the second floor.

They quickly eliminated the enemy fighters resisting on the first floor. As they arrived at the bottom of the stairs, Jared noticed the armory burning rapidly at the end of the hall. That wasn't the only thing he saw, as he raced down to where Staff Sergeant Hunter laid.

"Hunter, brother. Stay with us!"

Jared knelt down to where Hunter was laying, knowing the worst had occurred. As he checked

Hunter's pulse, it was confirmed. He was dead, defending his brothers to the very end. Refusing to leave him here, he began to try and pull him up, in order to carry him out. Struggling, he was hardly getting Hunter off the ground, when suddenly it became easy. As Jared got Hunter in a fireman's carry, he turned around to see Bashar helping him.

"Thank you Bashar."

No response, Bashar stepped out of Jared's way to let him through. There was still quite a few fighters outside that the General and his team were fighting off through the door and windows. They needed to get out quickly, as the building was rapidly burning down.

"We got to go," someone shouted.

"As soon as we step outside, they will shoot every single one of us," someone else shouted back.

Suddenly, a large thumping sound was in the air. As if a herd of elephants had ran in front of the building smashing everything in view. After ten seconds of this sound, everything quit. Peering out the window, the team discovered what happened.

Hunter's company commander had sent another quick reaction force to follow the General's convoy thirty minutes after they had left, to help relieve them if necessary. It was!

The large group of enemy fighters had been decimated by their heavy weapons, while all of their focus was on the building's front door. Jared and the team was able to exit the building before the fire destroyed the entire building. As they got to the open area in front of the building, the quick reaction force began to dismount their vehicles and provide security.

It was over. The Army of Islam was destroyed. Adir was dead, rid from this world no longer able to inflict pain and suffering to those that didn't deserve it. The General would talk to the region and assist the Ramadi government in regaining their power. Jared slowly turned and looked around the area, watching the building he had spent the last month and a half in burn to the ground. There was a tap on his shoulder. Jared turned around to see General Rogers standing there.

"Gunny, let's go home."

"Sounds like a plan to me Sir."

<u>CHAPTER TWENTY THREE</u>

The End

<u>*October 7th 2019*</u>

Jared was sitting on a black leather couch, staring out of a large window facing a beautiful treeline in the distance. They had arrived back in the states ten days ago. After about a week in Washington doing debriefs, Jared was cleared to go home and see his family. After this one last thing of course.

General Rogers walked through the door, entering his own office that Jared had already been sitting in, waiting. Jared stood up at attention as soon as he heard the door open.

"Good morning Sir!"

"Shut up and sit down Jared," came the response. Smiling, the General walked over to his desk pouring a drink. Turning around, he handed Jared a glass of whiskey. Jared took it from the General and sat back down, looking back through the window at the forest.

"So what now Jared? What's next for you, next for your career," General Rogers asked as he settled into his own chair behind his desk?

Jared didn't answer right away, not sure how to answer the question. He knew what he had to do, he just had no idea if they would let him.

"You know Sir, I have no idea what's next for me in my career. I wish I did, I just have no future thoughts on that topic. What I do know though, is that I want to go home. My kids need me, they need one of their parents to be around. They have had a rough year, and I think it's time I go home and be with them for a while."

The General stared at Jared for a minute before responding. Slowly, a tight smile crept across his face.

"Of course you would say that Jared, why wouldn't you. I expected that from the very beginning. That's why you have already been reassigned to work directly for me. My first assignment for you, is to go home for some much needed time. You will be on permissive duty until further notice. When your ready, let me know. You and your family can move here, to Washington. You will be my top advisor. This little stunt we pulled here got me my third star, which is all because of you."

General Rogers stood up and began to walk over towards Jared.

"When your ready, let me know. You want a promotion, done! You want to retire and work privately as a civilian, done. You let me know and I'll make it happen. No questions asked."

Jared stood up, reached out, and shook the Generals hand.

"Thank you Sir."

Jared turned around and walked towards the door. Grabbing the door with his right hand, he turned towards the General.

"I'll be in touch Sir!"

Jared walked through the door and shut it behind him. It was time to go home.

October 10th 2019

Sitting on the front porch of his new home in Tennessee, Jared was watching Cayden and Kaylee play in the front yard. They were smiling, having a great time. Albert and Linda were sitting there too, watching the kids play. He had just received news that Bashar had linked back up with his family. The Ramadi government was giving him some farm land to work directly for them and their export trade. Jared was in a good mood.

Jared looked around, noticing the beautiful sunset creeping through the sky. This used to be one of Katie's favorite things in the world. To sit out on the front porch and watch the world do its thing. He had a chair out there just for her, one that never got used.

"We are going to be alright Jared. These kids are tough, they get that from their mom," Linda spoke to Jared softly.

"Yes they do," Jared responded. "Yes they do. Everything is going to be ok."

Jared stood up and walked off the front porch. He did the one thing he looked forward too for the last several months. He went out to the front yard, where the sun was setting, and played with his kids.

Book 2

The American Terrorist

"Retaliation"

Preview

THE START

The field looked amazing, even though it wasn't a poppy field. However, after last year Bashar was given a substantial date farm that had been in existence for over fifteen years. One of the popular, legal exports for Iraq, Bashars assistance in getting the local government reinstated earned him and his family a new place to live with government work,

Bashar couldn't be happier. Adir and Asim was gone, the Army of Islam had been erased, other than the few remaining loyalist that were hiding for fear of prosecution. Bashar's family was ecstatic that he was still alive. Not to mention the American armies no longer harassed him over a date farm, owned by the government.

Bashar had woken up early, getting his truck ready to go check on the palms. As he grabbed a small snack that his wife had made him, he opened the door and started his volvo. Bashar pulled out though his gate, smiling as he began to drive down between palms full of dates.

Singing to himself, smiling from ear to ear, Bashar was excited about the state the dates were in. He felt as though he would have a good return this year, which was great for his first year out of captivity. Up ahead was his turn that led to the final edge of his field. Bashar slowed down, not wanting to tear up his soil within the field. Everything looked good on this end, time to head to the other side.

Suddenly the volvo was in the air, thrown by a small explosion. Bashar was flung from the side of the vehicle rolling out from the destroyed door. Rolling several times, Bashar felt pain through his entire body. Easing his head up from the ground, he looked down at his body. His left leg was mangled beyond recognition. A large piece of metal was sticking out of his right side. Blood was pooling around him on the ground. What had happened?

"Hello Bashar," came a voice?

Bashar couldn't raise himself up. He heard footsteps slowly walking towards him. A shadow crept across his head and upper torso. Turning his head to the right, Bashar seen a pair of black boots stepping around him. The feet walked towards Bashar's legs, coming into view.

"You!"

Bashar spit blood to the right said onto the ground, coughing slightly. Turning his head back, the man had a pistol aimed right at Bashar's face.

"I thought you had left the country," Bashar spoke softly.

"You didn't think I would come back for you. You must be as stupid as I thought you were when I first met you. What made you think I would allow you and that American traitor to kill my family, my father, after you had already killed my brother!"

Then he pulled the trigger

About The Author

Jeff served in the Marine Corps as an Infantry Machine Gunner and Unit Leader. His career spanned 5 deployments conducting operations in locations including Iraq, Afghanistan, and the Horn of Africa. His career includes numerous awards for valor, and the Purple Heart for wounds received in 2006 in Ramadi, Iraq.

In his writing career, Jeffrey has written content for many websites and blogs. He is the author of the three book Jared Tremble American Terrorist series

Jeff also manages his family's website, www.fromtumor2autism.com, sharing stories about their life regarding their journey as a military family with a son on the autism spectrum while living through a pediatric brain tumor.

Made in the USA
Columbia, SC
25 April 2022

59425461R00152